BIOS

TOR BOOKS BY ROBERT CHARLES WILSON

DARWINIA

BIOS

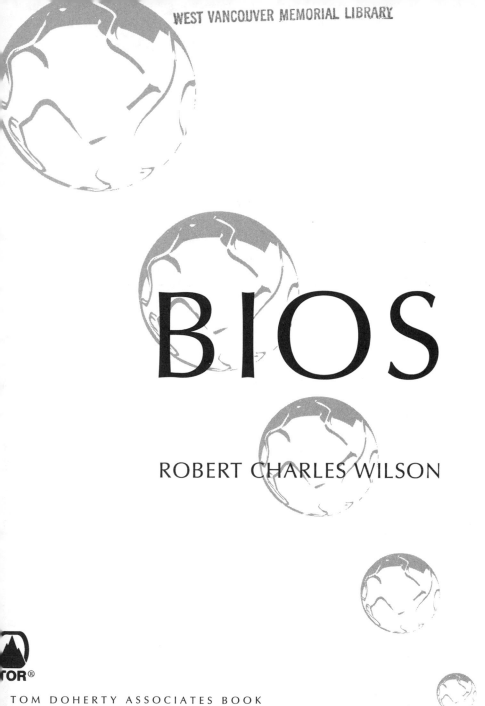

BIOS

ROBERT CHARLES WILSON

TOR®

A TOM DOHERTY ASSOCIATES BOOK
NEW YORK

BIOS

Copyright © 1999 by Robert Charles Wilson

Edited by Patrick Nielsen Hayden

A Tor Book
Published by Tom Doherty Associates, LLC
175 Fifth Avenue
New York, NY 10010

www.tor.com

Tor® is a registered trademark of Tom Doherty Associates, LLC.

Design by Lisa Pifher

Library of Congress Cataloging-in-Publication Data

Wilson, Robert Charles, 1953-
    Bios / Robert Charles Wilson.—1st ed.
      p.   cm.
    "A Tom Doherty Associates book."
    ISBN 0-312-86857-X (alk. paper)
    I. Title.
    PR9199.3.W4987B56   1999
    813'.54—dc21   99-37458
                        CIP

First Edition: November 1999

Printed in the United States of America

0 9 8 7 6 5 4 3 2 1

This one is for Sharry,
who saw me through.

PROLOGUE

THE REGULATOR LAY deep in the flesh of the girl's upper arm, a pale egg in a capillary nest.

Anna Chopra pared away the tissue with careful strokes of the hemostatic scalpel. Her small, expert hands wanted to tremble. She willed them to be steady.

This was, she knew, an act of sabotage. She was performing a surgical intervention without consent; worse, she was interfering with an instrument of the Trusts. Violating the law, if not, perhaps, her Hippocratic oath.

She was alone with the unconscious and sedated girl, and that had been part of the temptation. In any operating theater on Earth, she would have been surrounded by colleagues and students. On Earth, one was always surrounded. Here, at least for the moment, she was surrounded only by mute machinery and surgical tools dangling on coiled wire in the near-weightless environment. No audience, hence no witnesses: she was trustworthy, or so the Trusts believed.

The thymostat had been installed in the girl's arm years ago. It had gone about its business flawlessly and showed no sign of failing now. "The thermostat of the soul," her professor at Calcutta had called the common bioregulator. It was, in effect, an artificial gland, monitoring blood levels and maintaining self-synthesized doses of neurotransmitters and inhibitors—leveling moods, sustaining alertness, suppressing fatigue. Anna Chopra wore one herself, as did most Terrestrial technicians and managers.

But this girl—young woman really, though she looked like an infant from the perspective of Anna's seventy years—this Zoe Fisher was different. Zoe Fisher was a creation of the Devices and Personnel branch of the Trusts. She had been bred and modulated for her work on the distant world of Isis. She was, essentially, a human machine. Her bioregulation was spectacularly thorough; Anna did not doubt that the girl's every bad dream and brief ecstasy had been monitored, calculated, and soothed by this small but complex thymostat well before she learned to speak.

The bioregulator had put tendrils—samplers and drips—into the brachial artery and the ulnar collaterals. Anna Chopra severed the connections neatly and professionally, watching as the remnant pieces, self-suturing, merged into the artery's pulsing wall. The thymostat itself, about the size of a robin's egg and plump with blood, she pushed into the intake of a waste-disposal chute. Stray blood droplets drifted toward a gurgling air drain.

Why this small act of sabotage, why now? Maybe because a lifetime of obedience had left Anna Chopra feeling stale and futile. Maybe because this girl reminded Anna of her sisters, three of whom had been sold into the state brothels in Madras as a result of her family's financial reverses.

Brothel inmates were happy, everyone said—thoroughly trained and exhaustively bioregulated.

Young Zoe Fisher had probably never been near a brothel. But she was just as surely a slave, and her thymostat might as well have been a leg iron or a steel collar. Since she left Earth, Anna Chopra had met many technicians from the Kuiper Republics, none of whom wore regulators of any kind, and she had come to envy their spontaneity, their wealth of moods, their rawness. She might have been such a person herself, given the opportunity. Given another lifetime.

Let the Trusts find out what happened when one of their marionettes woke up without its strings.

Oh, most likely the theft would be detected and a new regulator installed. But maybe not. Zoe Fisher was bound for Isis—the farthest outpost of human exploration, far beyond even the isolated kibbutzim of the Kuiper Republics. A frontier, where the power of the Trusts was limited.

Anna Chopra closed the incision and sealed it with a gel rich in regenerative nanobacters. Finished with her act of sabotage—and instantly guilty about what she had done—Anna proceeded to her real work, rotating the girl's unconscious body in its surgical sling, cutting into the abdominal muscles to replace a depleted blood filter. Zoe was full of new technology, mainly immune-system enhancers of a kind Anna had never seen before. Bloody white biomodules clustered around the abdominal aorta like insect eggs on milkweed. Anna ignored these mysterious devices; she replaced the defective renal filter and closed the muscle tissue with more gel.

And was finished. She instructed the anesthistat, a hulking black tractible robot, to bring Zoe up to a natural sleep state and maintain the analgesic drip. At last she stripped off her gloves and stepped back from the surgical sling.

Now her hands began to shake in earnest. Anna's seventy years were about half the average lifetime of a senior manager or a member of the Families, but she was a mere Level Three technician and her telomerases were rapidly running out. According to her career schedule, she would be in a Terrestrial geriatric hospice before the end of the decade. Where she could allow her hands to tremble freely while she waited for degenerative disease or quota euthanasia to end her life—her functional, perfect life as a good citizen of the Trusts and servant of the Families.

Barring the occasional act of defiance.

She glanced reflexively over her shoulder, but of course there was no one to witness her criminal act. This small cometary object—they called it Phoenix—was very nearly uninhabited now. All but the vital staff had left in preparation for the Higgs launch. Nor was physical evidence a problem. Before very long, nothing would remain of Phoenix but scattered radioactive particles and Cherenkov radiation.

Embers and ashes. The thought was soothing, somehow. Her rapidly beating heart began to slow. All that persisted, Anna told herself, were embers and ashes, sparks and dust.

It was the Kuiper technicians who had named this planetisimal "Phoenix." Even a small world, they insisted, ought to have a name before it ceased to exist.

Phoenix rolled around the sun well beyond the orbit of Neptune and above the plane of the solar ecliptic—the desert of the solar system. In a matter of hours now, Phoenix would die in the most dramatic possible fashion. And when Phoenix vanished from the solar system, so would Zoe Fisher.

The technicians suiting Zoe for the launch seemed in awe of her, though they had rehearsed this act countless times. In awe, at least, of the forces to which Zoe would soon be subjected. If they could, Zoe thought, they would write their names on her body, like twentieth-century war pilots autographing a missile.

But she was not a missile. She was simply cargo. Five and a half feet and one hundred and thirty pounds of cargo. No different from the three other human beings, several hundred clonal mouse and pig embryos, and sundry supplies also bound for Isis. Soon enough, they would all be loaded into the catacombs of the Higgs sphere buried in the icy core of Phoenix.

The pre-launch supervisor—he was one of those long-faced Terrestrial kachos who serviced starships and their cargo but would never dare dream of riding one himself—approached Zoe where she sat half-embedded in her armor. His lips were pursed into a frown. "There's a call for you, Citizen Fisher."

This late in the launch sequence, Zoe thought, it must be

someone with a great deal of clout, someone highly placed in the Trusts or at least—dare she hope?—in the Devices and Personnel branch. The lower half of her body was already entombed in the bulky journeyrig, steel sheaths too massive to lift, under any kind of spin, without the help of powerful hydraulics. She felt like a knight-errant about to be winched onto her horse. Helpless. "Who is it?"

"Your D-and-P man from the Diemos installation."

Theo. Of course. She grinned. "Float me a monitor, please."

He made a sour face but brought her a screen. The suiting room was cramped, but so was every chamber inside the cometary fragment. Much of Phoenix had been excavated to contain the fusion launcher and payload, the small world's water-rich debris vectored off to reclamation points nearer the sun. These pressurized chambers were essentially makeshift—why waste labor on a habitat meant to be vaporized? The room around her was as stark as the Turing constructors had left it, medical and technical gear strapped randomly to the flat white walls.

At least her hands were free. Zoe touched a finger to the identity pad of the monitor.

Avrion Theophilus appeared at once. Theo was an older man, well into the first decade of his second century. His hair was white but thick, his skin pale but supple. He greeted her in High English, causing the Kuiper-born technicians to exchange uneasy looks.

He apologized for the interruption. "I wanted to wish you luck, not that you need it. Time is short, I know."

Too short. Or not short enough. Zoe couldn't name the odd hollowness she felt in her stomach. "Thank you."

She wished he could be here to say good-bye in person. She missed her mentor. She had left him more than a year ago, in a sun garden on Diemos. Theo couldn't come to Phoenix because he would have brought his intestinal flora with him. Phoenix was clean—at the moment, the cleanest inhabited environment in the system; Zoe's own benign bacteria and other biological hitchhikers had been systematically eradicated, replaced where necessary with sterile nanobacters. Even the technicians from the disease-free Kuiper colonies had been deconned for service on Phoenix.

"Be brave, little one," Theo said. "It looks crowded there."

The chamber *was* crowded, crowded with technicians as close as cattle in a pen, all of them waiting impatiently for Zoe to finish her conversation. "They treat me as if I'm radioactive," she whispered.

"You're not. But *they* will be, if they don't evacuate on schedule. I don't doubt it makes them nervous. We ought to let them get on with their work."

"I'm glad you called." It was good to see him again, his High Family face so calm and proud. Avrion Theophilus was the only human being Zoe had ever fully trusted, and the hardest part of this mission—at least so far—had been her separation from Theo. Was that a paradox? She had been bred and regulated to endure solitude. But Theo was different. He wasn't ordinary people. He was . . . well, *Theo.*

The closest thing to a father she had ever known.

"Travel safely, Zoe." He seemed to hesitate. "You know I envy you."

"I wish you could come with me."

"Someday. With any luck, someday soon."

That was cryptic, but Zoe didn't ask what he meant. Theo had always wanted to see Isis. And in a sense, he *was* going with her. You can't take much baggage across the bridge to the stars, Theo used to say. But memories were massless, and her memories of Theo were deeply held. She wanted to tell him so, but her throat closed on the words.

He gave her an encouraging smile and as suddenly as that, was gone. A technician took the monitor away.

Time ebbed quickly now. The journeyrig's containment ring snapped shut around her throat, immobilizing her head. This part would be uncomfortable, though she had rehearsed it a number of times; she would have to endure paralytic confinement and absolute darkness, at least until the medical system was activated and the suit began to flood her body with narcotic and anxiolytic molecules. I will sleep, Zoe thought, inside this steel box.

She waited for the massive helmet, dark and enclosing. Her heart hammered at the cage of her ribs.

The remaining technical staff, Anna Chopra among them, left Phoenix in a small armada of reaction rockets.

Anna had not forgotten her small act of defiance, though she wished she could. It had been, of course, stupid. A gesture, a whim, without utility, and in all likelihood without consequence. She was tempted to confess and have done with it; better an early euthanasia than another ten years in a geriatric ward.

Although . . . she took a deep and private pleasure at having, finally, at her age, a secret worth keeping.

Had she done the girl a favor? She had thought so when she applied scalpel to flesh, but she doubted it now. When Zoe Fisher woke up without her neurochemical safety net, the change would not be obvious. It would take weeks, perhaps months, for her neural receptors to perceive and react to the absence of the thymostat. Symptoms would set in gradually, maybe gradually enough for Zoe to adapt to the unregulated life. She might even learn to like herself that way. But sooner or later, the Trusts would find her out. Her thymostat would be replaced, and whatever new essence Zoe had distilled in herself would be drained away. And that would be that.

But, still . . . everything born had to die, the Trusts perhaps excluded, and if life meant anything, then even a brief life was better than none. Deep inside herself, Anna liked the idea of this Zoe Fisher, this Devices and Personnel bottle baby, wrenched out of the grip of the Trusts even for a day.

Do something, Zoe, Anna thought. Do something gaudy or foolish or grand. Weep, fall in love, write poetry. Look wild-eyed at this new world of yours.

She adjusted her cabin screen to the exterior view of Phoenix, already a faint point of light in a well of empty space. She had decided she wanted to see the launch—the bright bloom of the fusion event, the brilliant aurora as it faded.

Comatose and immobilized, Zoe became one more inert object to be ferried by tractible into the deep core of the launch facility and harnessed inside the payload sphere, which was suspended in turn by enormous pylons from the cored massif of rock and ice. Lenses of exotic matter surrounded the sphere like huge octagonal crystals. The lenses would be destroyed along with the rest of Phoenix, but only in the femtoseconds after they had served their purpose.

The cometary body was rigged for induced-field fusion. Neither Zoe nor the tractible robots were aware of the countdown ticking away in Phoenix's supercooled processor arrays. The detonation would be triggered by processors in the payload capsule itself as soon as the fail-safe sequences were satisfied.

It was the third interstellar launch this Terrestrial year, each launch as costly as creating an entire new Kuiper habitat or a Martian airfarm. A measurable fraction of the solar system's economic output had been channeled into this project. Not since the ancient days of *Apollo* and *Soyuz* had exploration been so enormously difficult to manage and finance.

All irreversible now. Microswitches poised for months fell at last into their final alignment.

Zoe slept, and if she dreamed, she dreamed only of motion, a separation as ponderous as the calving of glaciers.

In her dreams, the light was fiercely bright.

PART

ONE

ONE

DECANTED UNCONSCIOUS INTO the almost windowless environment of the Isis Orbital Station, Zoe longed for a glimpse of her new world. Wanted it so badly, in fact, that she was contemplating a serious breach of protocol.

She could prompt the image of Isis onto any local screen, of course. And she had seen such images for much of her life, often daily—images either relayed to Sol from the IOS or captured by the planetary interferometer.

But that wasn't enough. She was *here*, after all: scant hundreds of kilometers from the surface of the planet itself, Low Isis Orbit. She had traveled farther in an instant than a conventional spacefarer could hope to travel in a lifetime. She had arrived at the very edge of the human diaspora, the dizzying brink of the abyssal deeps, and she deserved a direct look at the planet that had drawn her so far from home—didn't she?

In the old days, astronomers had talked about "first light"— the fresh view through a brand-new optical instrument. Zoe had looked at Isis through every kind of optical instrument, barring her own eyes. Now she wanted that direct view, her own personal first light.

Instead, she had spent three days in the IOS's infirmary under useless observation and a week haunting her assigned cabin while waiting for a place on the duty roster. Ten days from decantation, ten days without orders, agenda, or more than a brief word from management. She had seen to date only the gently concave walls and steel floors of her cubby and the recovery ward in Medical. The sole official communications she had received were a list of meal hours, an access code, her residence number, and a name badge.

Consequently, Zoe summoned her courage and scheduled an appointment with Kenyon Degrandpre, the outpost manager. She was awed at her own impertinence. Probably she should have talked to her section chief first . . . but no one had told her who her section chief was or how to find him.

The Isis Orbital Station had been assembled from the shells of early model Higgs spheres in a ring-of-pearls configuration. The maps posted on the corridor walls reminded Zoe of the benzene rings illustrated in chemistry texts, with the outpost's fusion bottles and heat exchangers projecting like complex side chains from the symmetrical core. On the morning of her appointment with Degrandpre, Zoe left her tiny cabin at the bottom of Habitat Seven and walked the ring corridor a kilometer spinward, nearly half the total circumference of the IOS. The ring corridor smelled of hot metal and cycled atmosphere, like a Kuiper habitat, but without the ever-present tang of ice in the air. Bulkhead doors loomed like massive guillotine blades; the gangways were narrow and possessed neither charm nor windows. This place was not as emotionally and culturally blank as Phoenix had been, but neither was it a typical Kuiper world, full of color and noisy with children. The Terrestrial esthetic prevailed: linear functionality, enforced by strict cargo limitations.

Windows were a luxury, Zoe supposed. According to the IOS plan she'd reviewed on her terminal, the project manager's office possessed one of the station's few accessible direct-view windows, a wedge of three-inch-thick polarized glass set into the exterior wall. The rest of the station's windows were tiny ports cut into the docking bays, an area for which Zoe was not yet authorized. But that was irrelevant, she told herself. She had business with Degrandpre. The window was just . . . a perquisite.

From the name, she had expected someone almost Family—weren't there Degrandpres among the Brazilian landholders?—but Kenyon Degrandpre was not a handsome or an imposing man. A manager of some rank, but never Family. His head was too long, his nose too flat. Zoe's experience with the upper echelons of the Trusts had taught her that handsome managers might be capable of a certain generosity; ugly men—although Degrandpre didn't quite fit that description either, at least not by Terrestrial standards—were more likely to read regulations and nurse grudges. She knew for a fact, had known all her life, that rigid personalities were a staple in the bureaucracies of the Trusts. But surely the man who managed the Isis Orbital Station, in effect the Isis Project itself, must be more flexible. Mustn't he?

Maybe not. Degrandpre raised his big head briefly and waved Zoe to a chair, but his attention remained on his desktop.

Zoe stood near the window instead. It wasn't much of a window. She supposed the brutal payload limitations of the Higgs launchers made even this small luxury prohibitively expensive. Still, here was her first genuinely direct view of the planet below. Unmediated light, Zoe thought excitedly. *First* light.

The IOS had just crossed the planet's terminator. The long light of dawn picked out clouds in vivid chiaroscuro. Across the dark zone, lightning flickered, embers on velvet.

Zoe had seen planets before. She had seen Earth from orbit, a view not dissimilar. She'd spent a year on Europa learning pressure lab technique, and the vast orb of Jupiter had filled more of the sky far more dramatically.

But this was *Isis*. That glitter of sunlight came from a star not

Earth's. Here was a living world that had never seen a naked human footprint, a world strange and alive, rich with biology; a swarming waterdrop orbiting a foreign sun. As lovely as Earth. And infinitely more deadly.

"Is there an issue," Degrandpre said at last, "or have you come to stare? You wouldn't be the first, Citizen Fisher."

Degrandpre's voice had the bite of Terrestrial authority. His English was finely honed. Zoe thought she heard a touch of Beijing Elite School in the understated consonants.

She took a breath. "I've been here ten days. Apart from the Habitat Seven physical regime director and the cafeteria staff, I haven't spoken to anyone in authority. I don't know who to report to. The people who are supposed to oversee my work directly are all on-planet—which is where I ought to be."

Degrandpre tapped his stylus and sat back in his chair. His clothing was sere gray, the inevitable kacho uniform, a stiff black collar framing his thick peasant neck. Wooden chair, wooden desk, a plush carpet, and a multilayered dress uniform; all of this would have been shipped from Earth, at an expense Zoe shuddered to consider. He asked, "Do you feel neglected?"

"No, not neglected. I just wanted to make certain—"

"That we haven't forgotten you."

"Well . . . yes, Manager."

Degrandpre continued to tap his stylus against the desktop, a sound that made Zoe think of ice cracking in a warm glass. He seemed as much amused as irritated. "Let me ask you this, Citizen Fisher. In an outpost of this size, with every gram accounted for and every sou budgeted, do you really suppose people get *lost?*"

She reddened. "I wasn't thinking of it that way."

"In the last six weeks, we've conducted four shuttle exchanges with the downstations. Each exchange calls for lengthy quarantine and elaborate sterile docking protocols. Flights are scheduled months in advance. You people arrive thinking the Higgs launch was the bottleneck and that a trip downside must be a holiday jaunt by comparison. Not so. I'm aware of your presence and your purpose, and you have a place, obviously, on the rotation list. But our first priority has to be resupply and maintenance. You must understand that."

But you knew I was coming, Zoe thought. Why didn't the schedule reflect that? Or had there been delays she didn't know about? "Beg pardon, Manager Degrandpre, but I haven't even seen an agenda. When am I scheduled to drop?"

"You'll be notified. Is that all?"

"Well . . . yes, sir." Now that she'd looked through the window.

Degrandpre eyed his rapidly scrolling desktop. "I have a delegation from Yambuku waiting outside. People you'll be working with. You might as well stay and listen. Meet your colleagues." He said this as if he had made a grand concession. Planned, of course, in advance. It was one of those kacho maneuvers the bureaucrats loved so much. Surprise the opposition; never *be* surprised.

Zoe said, "Yambuku?"

"Downstation Delta. Delta is called Yambuku; Gamma is Marburg."

"Yambuku" and "Marburg" were the first identified strains of the hemorrhagic fever that had devastated twenty-first-century Earth. A microbiologist's joke. Most likely a Kuiper microbiologist's joke. The Terrestrial sense of humor was limited in that department.

"Sit," Degrandpre said. "Pay attention. Try not to talk. You may continue looking out the window if you like."

She ignored his sarcasm and did exactly that.

Dawn had reached the scattered island chains of the Western Sea. A dark plume of ejecta, like soot, trailed from an active volcano. The Greater Continental Mass wheeled into view, dense with temperate and boreal forests. Sunlight glinted from an ancient blue crater lake here, glanced off a fringe of polar ice there. Cloudtops white as cut diamonds.

And all of it as lethal as arsenic.

Her new home.

.   .   .

Two men and a woman shuffled into the room and occupied the conference table. Zoe continued to linger by the window. She didn't need Degrandpre's advice to keep quiet; she found crowded rooms intimidating.

Kenyon Degrandpre introduced the new arrivals as Tam Hayes, Elam Mather, and Dieter Franklin, all from Yambuku Station, all up on the latest shuttle.

Zoe recognized Hayes from photos. He was the Delta station manager and the Isis Project's senior biologist—senior in status, not in age. Hayes was a relatively young man despite his five years on Isis rotation, handsome in a rough way. He needed a haircut, Zoe thought. His beard was like tangled copper. A typical disheveled Kuiper-born scientist, in other words. The other two weren't much different.

Hayes thrust his hand at her. "Zoe Fisher! We were hoping to meet you."

Zoe took his hand reluctantly. She didn't like touching people. Hadn't Hayes been briefed on that, or didn't he care? Her hand disappeared into his meaty grip. "Dr. Hayes," she murmured, concealing her uneasiness.

"Please, call me Tam. I gather we'll be working together."

"You can get to know each other later," Degrandpre said. To Zoe: "Dr. Hayes and his people have been vetting proposed archival material for transmission to Earth."

Zoe followed the exchange between Hayes and Degrandpre closely, trying to sort out the conflicts. The particle-pair link to Earth was such a narrow pipeline, so severely bandwidth-limited, that project downloads were hotly contested and had to undergo a kind of information triage. Degrandpre was the final arbiter. So here was Hayes, the Yambuku project leader, delivering an impatient summary of his group's packet data, and Degrandpre playing the infuriating role of ultimate Trust bureaucrat: aloof, bored, skeptical. He fiddled with his stylus and crossed his legs and periodically asked Hayes to clarify some point that had been perfectly obvious to begin with. Finally he said, "Show me the visuals." Holographs and photos were particularly expensive to transmit, but they took the place of voucher specimens and were often popular in the press back home.

A large central screeen unfurled from the ceiling.

The images in the Yambuku packet were micrographs of viruses, bacteria, prions, and biologically active protein chains, all of them "ALC," as Hayes put it: Awaiting Latin Cognomen. There was also a series of conventional photographs to illustrate a journal submission from one of his junior biologists. Degrandpre asked, "More exploding mice?"

Zoe had never heard the expression.

Judging by the look on his face, Hayes disliked it. "Live-animal exposures, yes."

"Ramp them up, please, Dr. Hayes."

Hayes used a handheld scroll to order up the images from the IOS's central memory. Zoe caught Degrandpre glancing at her curiously. Gauging her reaction? If so, why?

Elam Mather, a thick-faced woman in lab grays, stood up to narrate the images. Her voice was strong and impatient.

"The concept here was to sort ambient Isian microorganisms through a series of micron filters in order to evaluate their lethality and mode of action. We took a sample of air from outside the station, near dusk on a calm, dry day. Meteorological notes are appended. Crude assay gave us a load of organic matter and the usual assortment of water droplets, silicate dust, and so forth. One sample was forced through a filter and injected into an isolation chamber containing a clonal mouse of the CIBA-thirty-seven strain."

An image came up on the screen.

Zoe looked at it, swallowed, and looked away.

"The result," Elam Mather said, "was essentially the same as for unfiltered native air. Within minutes, the mouse had spiked a fever and before two hours had passed it was bleeding internally. Systemic collapse, bleedout and tissue deliquescence followed rapidly. More than a dozen foreign microbial species were cultured from the mouse's blood; again, the usual suspects.

"The next sample went through a finer screening. On Earth,

that would remove all spores and bacteria, but not viruses or prions.

"The second exposed mouse also died—obviously—but the onset of the toxemia was slightly more gradual. The outcome, however, was the same."

A mix of fur and muscle tissue in a pool of deliquescent black liquid. The CIBA-37 mouse might as well have been popped into a food processor. Probably, Zoe thought, that would have been kinder.

The sight of the dead creature affected her more than she expected. Her throat constricted and she wondered if she might have to vomit.

She narrowed her eyes in order to avoid the rest of the photographs while pretending to look at them. The research duplicated, confirmed, and extended earlier work; there was nothing very novel about it. Either Degrandpre had wanted to see it himself, or he had wanted Zoe to see it.

Because I'm not a microbiologist, Zoe thought. He sees me as some pampered Terrestrial theoretician. As if I didn't know what I was getting into!

"Even with microfine HEPA filtration, clonal mice eventually sickened after repeated exposure to native air. In this case, we're looking at dusts and protein fragments perhaps triggering an allergenic reaction, not the full hemorrhagic blowout, but still a deadly hazard. . . ."

The man named Dieter Franklin said laconically, "The planet is trying to kill us. But we proved that long ago. The surprising thing is how *hard* it's trying to kill us."

Degrandpre shot Zoe one more glance, as if to say, "You see? Isis will kill you if you let it."

Zoe remained expressionless. She didn't want to give him the satisfaction of knowing she was afraid.

She ran into Tam Hayes in the cafeteria a day later.

The cafeteria was as spartan as every other chamber in the

IOS—steel deck assembled by Turing constructors, welded seams exposed, the chairs and trestle tables flimsy and makeshift. This was inevitable in an environment where every manufactured object was either shipped in from Earth at obscene expense or pieced together by Turing factories on Isis's Diemos-sized moon. At least the cafeteria had been decorated. Some artistic soul had grooved the flat inner walls with an assembly etcher, wasting time and energy, Zoe supposed, but not essential supplies. The far wall was a Celtic tapestry of knotted lines, with Kuiper clan signs worked discreetly into the design. Pretty enough, she thought, if vaguely subversive.

Unfortunately, the overhead lights were naked sulfur-microwave dots; they made the food look as bright and false as polystyrene.

" 'Morning, Dr. Fisher." Hayes came up behind her carrying a thermal bowl of glutinous flavinoid soup. "Mind if I join you?"

"Morning?" Dinnertime, by Zoe's clock.

"I'm keeping Yambuku time. Sun's just coming up over the lowlands, unless it's raining. You'll see it soon enough yourself."

"I'm looking forward to it. I haven't seen much from orbit."

"They're stingy with windows. But the live relays are almost as good."

"I saw camera feeds back home."

He nodded. "IOS fever. I know the feeling. Suffered from it myself once." He settled into a chair opposite her. "You want the real thing. But Yambuku's much the same, I'm afraid. Isis is right there under your feet, but you're still utterly isolated from it. Sometimes I dream of walking outside—without excursion armor, I mean." He added, "I envy you, Dr. Fisher. Sooner or later, you'll have that experience."

"Call me Zoe." He obviously preferred Kuiper-style informality or he wouldn't be here talking to her.

He offered his hand—again. She took it reluctantly. His hand was dry; hers was moist. He said, "I'm Tam."

She knew all about him from her prep reading. Hayes ran Yambuku from the ground. He was a technical manager and microbiologist, exiled from some puritanical Kuiper colony because he had dared to sign a contract with the Trusts.

He was thirty-five years old. Real years: he hadn't taken rejuvenation treatments. Zoe found herself drawn to the wrinkles at the corners of his eyes, amiable contour maps. Like Theo's eye lines, but less harsh, less etched.

"You envy me," she said, "but Kenyon Degrandpre seems to think I'm doomed."

"Well, Degrandpre. . . . IOS politics mean nothing to me, but Degrandpre is old Terrestrial stock. No insult intended. He's a manager, a kacho. He'd be happy if nothing ever changed here. Keep the equilibrium, balance the books, save face, that's his agenda. Don't expect sympathy from Kenyon Degrandpre."

"It seemed like he was trying to frighten me."

"Did it work?"

He meant the remark jokingly, but Zoe was startled.

Because, yes. She *was* frightened.

She was, now that she came to admit it, so frightened that the food stuck in her throat and her stomach clenched like a fist.

More frightened than she had thought possible.

"Zoe?" Hayes frowned across the table. "Are you all right?"

She controlled herself. "Yes."

Just waiting for her thymostat to do its work, to wash her in some soothing bath of neurotransmitters. It would happen, Zoe was sure, if she was only patient enough. The fear would go away, and she would be normal again.

TWO

TRAVELING BACK TO the surface of Isis was ordinarily a tedious process, at least in calm weather—and better tedious
than exciting—but the shuttle had barely broken the cloud
layer when Tam Hayes discovered he had a crisis waiting for him.
Not that a crisis was unusual at Yambuku, either. But this crisis
might prove lethal.

Hayes had left Macabie Feya in charge of the station. Mac was
an accomplished engineer, a Reformed Mormon, Needle Clan out
of Kuiper Body 22, with a genius for micro and Turing devices
and as fine a grasp of sterile technique as a Kuiper education could
provide. He was also an old Yambuku hand with two years' station
time behind him, and he should have known better than to venture
outside with uncertified armor. But that was exactly what Mac had
done, and he had got himself into trouble out in open air.

A scatter of cirrus ran high across the western steppes. The
shuttle skimmed through overcast into watery daylight. Winds
were light, though a distant storm cell dropped curtains of rain a

dozen kilometers north of the river valley. Eastward, the Copper Mountain range was all but invisible in an upwash of cloud; a few fingers of sunlight touched the emerald foothills. Yambuku was situated in a relatively dry forested incline in the heart of the Western Continent, but Isis was everywhere a wet world. The rains came almost daily and winds were often a problem, complicating shuttle schedules and shutting down mobile remotes.

Hayes moved up next to the shuttle's reserve pilot, who nodded curtly. "Not much in the way of details so far, Dr. Hayes. They're pretty busy with this. I gather Mac Feya was outside the station doing maintenance and he suffered some kind of suit breach . . . not a full breach, but they're hung up on decon, plus he's stuck in place with an armor malfunction."

"Just get me there," Hayes said.

"Doing our best."

Yambuku's docking bay was the largest structure associated with the station. A domed vault rising above the station's sterile core, it opened for the shuttle's vertical landing and closed, agonizingly slowly, over the landing pad. The Isian atmosphere was evacuated and flushed with sterile air from the exchange stacks; then the chamber was triple-washed with aerosol sterilants, ultraviolet light, and radiant heat not much less searing than the reentry burn had been. During the interminable washdown, Hayes spoke with Cai Connor, ops chief while Hayes was absent and Mac was incapacitated.

Connor, an organic chemist, was almost as seasoned a hand as Mac Feya. Hayes didn't doubt she was handling the emergency at least as well as he would have, but he heard the catch of anxiety in her voice. "Contact with Mac is sporadic. We have remote tractibles with him, but he's noncooperative. The decon is going to be tricky at best, and we don't want to force a joint and open another breach—"

"Take a breath, Cai. From the beginning, please. All I know is that Mac was out on a maintenance excursion."

"It was another seal failure, this one on the south tractible bay. You know how these ring faults have been driving Mac crazy. Frankly, he shouldn't have gone out. The alpha excursion suit was hung up in maintenance, so he took the beta unit even though it hasn't been through a refit since the last walkabout. I guess it needed it. He was at the bay door taking samples from the bad seal and laying down a caulk bead when a servo in his right leg over-heated. Suit homeostasis went crazy, then that system locked too. Big, big cascade failure. The servomotor fused a hole through the exterior armor, and the inner seal may or may not have been breached—we have contradictory telemetry on that. But it for sure cooked Mac's leg above the knee. He's in pain even with the suit feeding him analgesics, and the analgesics are about to run out. Plus, he's incoherent, so we can't count on him cooperating with any rescue effort."

Hayes winced. God help Mac, riveted to the ground by a bad motor, seared and in pain, not knowing—and this must be the worst of it—whether his bioperimeter was intact or whether he was already, in effect, a dead man. "Cai, how deep in maintenance is the alpha suit?"

"Hang on." She consulted someone away from the transducer. "I fast-tracked it as soon as Mac's alarms sounded. It's been through preliminary diagnostics and looks okay, but none of the deep testing has gone ahead."

"Pull it out and prep it."

"That might not be wise."

"Prep it, Cai, thank you. And get the tunnel out here."

"Okay, it's happening." She sounded relieved to have him back in charge, despite her misgivings. "You're about twenty minutes away from confirmation."

"I want the armor prepped as soon as I'm through the tunnel. In the meantime, do whatever you were doing—keep Mac as calm as possible and have the tractibles handy with a chordal brace. And relay his telemetry, let me see if I can make sense of it."

"Yes," she said promptly. Station rank was informal. Cai, a Kuiper freewoman of the purest sort, would never call him "Sir," the way Terrestrial scientists inevitably did. But he heard the deference in her voice.

And felt the burden of responsibility shift squarely onto his own shoulders.

The new hand—Zoe Fisher, the bottle baby whose novel excursion suit was still deep in stowage, unfortunately—came forward from the passenger cabin. She was solemn, frowning. "Is there anything I can do?"

"You can keep out of the way." It was the first thing that came to mind.

She nodded once and left the cabin.

Hang on, Mac, Hayes thought.

Yambuku didn't need another tutelary death. Isis had claimed too many lives already.

Isis's day averaged three hours longer than Earth's, and its axial tilt was less acute, the seasons milder. The sun hovered above the Copper Mountains as Hayes, encased in an impossibly bulky mass of bioarmor, left Yambuku. The surrounding forest was already dense with shadow; the long Isian nightfall was about an hour away.

A vast swath of vegetation had been cleared around the ground station, the soil burned and salted with long-lasting herbicides. Yambuku, its core and its four coaxial rings, sat embedded in this blackened wasteland like a lost pearl. The burn zone prevented native plants from overgrowing the station's pressed-aggregate walls, fouling the exits and weakening the seals. But it reminded Hayes of something else: the empty space between a fortress and a bailey; a field of fire.

It did nothing to deter airborne microorganisms—probable cause of the continuing seal failures—and already the weeds were beginning to make advances, green creepers twining out of the forest canopy like tentative fingers.

Hayes, sweating inside his isolation suit, felt the familiar sensation of being *in* the landscape but not *of* it. Every sensation—the crackle of scorched soil under his feet, the whisper of wind-tossed leaves—was relayed by suit sensors. His touch was blunted by the armor's fat gloves, sensitive and versatile though they were; his field of vision was blinkered, his sense of smell nonexistent. This river valley was as lush and wild as a summer garden, but he could never enter it except as proxy, robot, half-man.

It would, of course, kill him at the first opportunity.

He passed the curved wall of the station, rising like a limestone cliff in the slanting sunlight, and reached the area outside the tractible port where Macabie Feya was trapped in his malfunctioning armor.

The problem was instantly obvious. Mac's right leg had burned out below the hip, leaving a flaring, blackened gap in the outer shield. Primary and secondary hydraulics were hopelessly damaged below the waist. He was locked in place, frozen in an awkward crouch.

The accident had happened almost eight hours ago. The suit itself had tourniqueted the leg and would even, if necessary, provide CPR and cardiostimulants; it was a good machine, even with its torso systems terminally cooked. But eight hours was a long time to be injured and alone. And the suit's modest reservoir of analgesics and narcotics was close to exhaustion.

Hayes approached his injured friend cautiously. The suit's legs might be locked down, but the powerful arms remained mobile. If Mac panicked, he could inflict serious damage.

Two land-duty tractibles rolled out of the way as Hayes came closer, cams glancing between Hayes and Macabie. Their eyes, of course, were Yambuku's eyes. Elam's eyes, in fact: Elam Mather was working the remotes. And how calm it all seemed in the late afternoon quiet, aviants chattering high in the trees, a black noonbug ambling across the ash-dark clearance like some tiny Victorian banker. Hayes cleared his throat. "Mac? Can you hear me?"

His voice was relayed by radio to Mac's headset. We hear the insects more clearly than we hear each other, Hayes thought. Two solitudes, semaphores across a microbiotic ocean.

There was no answer beyond the low hum of the carrier. Mac must have slipped back into unconsciousness.

Hayes was close enough now to examine the suit breach. The suit was multilayered, its hydraulics and motors normally operating in isolation from both their moist human cargo and the abrasive Isian biosphere. The overheat had peeled back the outer layer of flexarmor like foil, exposing a tangle of burned insulation and leaking blue fluids—a robot's wound. The soft nugget of Mac Feya lay deeper inside, hidden but horribly endangered.

Hayes needed Mac's cooperation—or else he needed Mac safely unconscious. He queried Elam about the telemetry.

"Far as I can tell, Tam, his vitals are as stable as we can expect. You want me to tell the suit to lighten his narcs?"

"Take his drip down just a notch, please, Elam."

"Sure you don't want to splint him first?"

"I'm already on it."

He unhooked a body brace from the nearest tractible and began linking it to Mac's upper-body armor. The tractibles could have done this themselves if they had been larger or more flexible. But this was Isis, and some Terrestrial kacho had written weight and size limitations into the robot inventory without thinking much about the practical consequences. Hayes worked from behind Mac, socketing the brace into chordal ports, the brace exchanging protocols with the suit's surviving electronics.

The link was almost complete when Mac woke up.

His scream rang through Hayes' helmet, a sound he did not immediately identify with his friend Macabie Feya. It was an inhuman roar, overwhelming the audio transducers. Elam shouted over it: "His vitals are spiking! He's not stable—you have to override his armor *now!*"

Grimly, Hayes forced the last brace connector into its socket on Mac's thrashing armor.

He was still trying to latch the device when Mac's elbow butted into him.

Hayes staggered backward, hurt and breathless. His armor was bulky but in its own way fragile, designed to protect him from the biosphere, not from physical attack. His ribs hurt, the breath was knocked out of him, and he heard the suit alarm clamoring for his attention.

"Tam, you have an outer-layer breach! Get back in the airlock, stat!"

"Mac," Hayes said.

The engineer's wordless keening dropped to a lower note.

"Mac, you can hear me, can't you?"

Elam: "Don't do this, Tam!"

"Mac, listen. You're doing fine. I know you're worried, and I know you've been out here too long, and I know you're in pain. We're about ready to haul you inside. But you have to relax, keep still a little longer."

There was a response this time, something about being "fucking trapped."

"Listen to me," Hayes said. He took a cautious step forward, keeping himself within Mac's visual range, gloves forward and open. "There's a brace on you, but it's not socketed up. I have to make the connection before we can take you inside."

Elam, still hammering him: "I cannot guarantee your suit integrity unless you get back here *now*!"

He took another step closer.

"I think you broke one of my ribs, Mac. Take it easy, all right? I know it hurts. But we're almost home, buddy."

Mac croaked something repetitive, choking on the words.

"You understand me, Mac?"

There was a silence he took for assent. Hayes grasped the brace jack in one glove, taking advantage of what he hoped was a moment of lucidity.

Mac reared back as the connection was made. Then the brace electronics overrode his voluntary functions, clamping his arms at his sides in full static lockdown. The motion must have been painful. Mac howled at his sudden new helplessness, an awful sound.

Two small tractibles approached, clasped the wings of the brace, and tilted it neatly backward. Now Mac was a wheeled vehicle, already rolling toward the tractible bay's outer decon chamber. Hayes kept pace, ignoring Elam's voice in his ear, staying where Mac could see him, keeping the injured man company until the bay doors rolled down on the deepening blue of the Isian dusk.

Hayes put his helmet against Mac's as the harsh station lights came up.

Mac whispered. The words—as nearly as Hayes could make out—were, "Too late."

He kept his helmet against Mac's as the decon began, caustic antiseptics misting from the ceiling in a pale green rain. Mac stared back at him through moist glass.

Hayes gave him a thumbs-up, hoping the insincerity of it wasn't ridiculously obvious.

Mac's eyes were blank and bloodshot. His pores leaked blood in ruby teardrops. Tissue deliquescence and bleedout had already begun.

Macabie Feya was dying, and there was nothing Hayes could do about it.

THREE

O N TOP OF everything else, there was the question of how to spin this unfortunate death.

The problem preoccupied Kenyon Degrandpre as he reported for his monthly medical evaluation. He was eager to speak to the doctor. Not that he was ill. But the senior medical manager—Corbus Nefford, a Boston-born physician with a long career in the Trusts—was also the closest thing to a friend Degrandpre had found aboard the IOS. Nefford, unlike the cold-world barbarians who dominated the scientific crew, understood the rules of civil discourse. He was friendly but mindful of the subtleties of rank, deferential but seldom distastefully toadying. Nefford possessed a chubby, aristocratic face that must have served him well in the professional sweepstakes back home; he looked like a Family cousin even in his modest physician's smock.

Degrandpre stepped into the small medical station and stripped unselfconsciously. Like his uniform, his body was an expression of rank and class. He was nearly hairless, his excess body fat chelated away, his musculature defined but not boastful. He wore a Works Trust tattoo on his left shoulder. His slender penis dangled over the faint scar of his orchidectomy, another badge of rank. He stepped quickly into the diagnostic nook.

Nefford sat attentively at his monitor, never so gauche as to speak before he was addressed.

Machinery hummed behind Degrandpre's back, a whisper of hummingbird wings. He said, "Of course you've heard about the death."

The physician nodded. "A suit breach, I gather. Tragic for the Yambuku staff. I suppose they'll have to replace the armor."

"Not to mention the engineer."

"Macabie Feya. Arrived thirty months ago. Healthy as a horse, but they all are, at least when they first set foot on the IOS. He caused the accident himself, I hear."

"He was in open air in poorly prepped protective gear. In that sense, yes, he brought it on himself. But fault has a way of rising up the ranks."

"Surely no one could blame you, Manager."

"Thank you for the unconvincing show of support. Of course we both know better."

"It's not an ideal world."

"We've lost two assets that will be expensive to replace. There's no way to finesse that. However, Yambuku is far from crippled. They can still make vehicular excursions, most of their tractibles are in decent shape, and they have at least one suit of bioarmor that can be brought up to specification fairly quickly. Basic research won't be interrupted."

"And," Nefford said, "they have the new gear that Fisher woman brought with her."

"Is that common knowledge?"

"For better or worse. The IOS is a village. People talk."

"Too much and too often." But Degrandpre expected a certain amount of gossip from Corbus Nefford. Because he was a physician and a section manager, Nefford's rice bowl was virtually ensured.

He could risk saying things others might keep to themselves. "What Zoe Fisher brought with her is an unproven technology foisted on us by a rogue branch of the Trusts. The Fisher woman comes with a vade mecum from Personnel and Devices, and she's putting herself directly in harm's way. That worries me. One death is attrition; two would look like incompetence—on someone's part."

The doctor nodded absently, whispering into his scroll. "The diagnostic's finished. Step down, please."

Degrandpre dressed himself, still thinking aloud. "Personnel and Devices act like they can shuffle our priorities at will. I doubt the Works commissioners will put up with this kind of arrogance much longer. In the meantime, I'd like Zoe Fisher to survive at least until I'm safely back in Beijing. It's not my battle, frankly." Had he overstepped? "This is privileged, of course."

"Of course."

"Not galley gossip, in other words."

"You know you can trust me, Kenyon." He used the given name not as an impertinence but with downcast eyes, to ingratiate.

"Thank you, *Corbus.*" A gentle rebuke. "So? Am I healthy?"

Nefford turned with visible relief to his desktop. "Your bone calcium is excellent, your musculature is stable, and your accumulated radiation exposure is well within tolerance. But next time, I want a blood sample."

"Next time, you may have one."

Once every calendar month, Degrandpre walked the circumference of the orbital station, from docking bays to sun garden, his left hand on the holster of his quirt.

He thought of the walkthrough as a way of staying in touch with the IOS. Keeping the maintenance crew on their toes, citing Works staff for uniform violations—in general, making his presence felt. (In the case of dress-code infringements, he had long ago given up on the Kuiper and Martian scientists; he considered himself lucky if they remembered to dress at all.) Problems that seemed distant from his chambers loomed larger from the deckplates. And he liked the exercise.

Invariably, he started his inspection at the dimly lit cargo-storage spaces of Ten Module and finished back at Nine, the garden. He liked to linger in the garden. If he had been asked, he might have said he enjoyed the filtered sunlight, pumped from fixed collectors in the IOS's hub, or the moist air, or the earthy smell of the aeroponic suspensions. And all that was true. But not all of the truth.

To Kenyon Degrandpre, the garden was a kind of pocket paradise.

He had loved gardens even as a child. For the first twelve years of his life he had lived with his father, a senior manager at the Cultivar Collection in southern France. The Collection's greenhouses ranged over thousands of acres of rolling pastureland, foundations tilted to the southern sky, a city of damp glass walls and hissing aerators.

"Paradise" was his father's name for it. In biblical mythology, paradise was a garden called Eden; the Edenic world was cultivated, perfect. When humankind fell from grace, the garden succumbed to anarchy.

On the IOS the garden was even more central, as delicate and vital as a transplanted heart. It supplied most of the station's nutritional needs; it recycled wastes; it cleansed the air. Because the garden was both indispensable and fragile, it was, at least in Degrandpre's eyes, the paradise of the Old Testament restored: orderly, calculated, organic, and precise.

The gardeners, in their buff fatigues, acknowledged his presence by staying out of his way. He walked the garden tiers slowly, pausing in a glade of tall tomato plants to savor the smell and the leaf-green light.

He had entered the Works with much of his father's idealism still intact. Humanity had endured a wild Earth for too long. The price had been uncontrolled population growth, climatic devolution, disease.

Kuiper radicals accused Earth of wallowing in stasis. Nonsense,

Degrandpre thought. How long would a Kuiper habitat or a Martian airfarm last if it failed to regulate its ice and oxygen mining? How long could the IOS, for instance, sustain itself in a state of anarchy? But there was nothing special about the surface of Earth; the issues were the same, only broader, more diffuse. Consider Isis itself: a garden never cultivated. Beautiful, as freshly arrived Kuiper enthusiasts never failed to point out. And fundamentally hostile to human life.

He passed through the vegetable gardens and climbed a flight of stairs to a terrace where delicately engineered fruit vines thrived near the light. Gardeners and slim white tractibles moved like angels among the lush foliage, and he savored the patient sound of dripping water. Home, Degrandpre found himself thinking: five years now since he'd seen it, and God knows what had gone on during his absence. The disastrous North African Aquifer Initiative had nearly cost him his career; he had called in every outstanding favor just to save his Works card. He had accepted the Isis rotation to demonstrate his adaptability. It was the only post of any responsibility he had been offered.

And he hadn't done badly here. But too much time had passed too slowly, and he felt the separation from Earth more keenly than he had expected. It was as if his body registered on the cellular level every inch of the vast distance the Higgs launcher had transected; he was, after all, so far from home that the sunlight falling on these vines would not reach Beijing or Boston or the south of France within his lifetime. His only real connection with the planet of his birth was the particle-pair link—a thin reed indeed.

But one to which he was obliged to attend. His weekly report was due. He would have to let the Trusts know that one of their engineers had died.

Bad luck. Or bad management. Or Kuiper adventurism gone wrong. Yes, that was it.

By midday, he had queued his report for transmission and was tending to other business. A summit of section managers arrived

bearing grievances: unfair tractible allotment and resource utiliza-
tion, the usual departmental jealousies. The Turing factories on
Isis's small moon had fallen short of productivity goals, though
another two factory units had been genned. The question was one
of balance. No one would get what he wanted, but that was inevitable. The IOS was an economy of scarcity.

The good news was that no truly critical shortages were pressing, Turing productivity had increased even if it had not met ex-
pectations, and the IOS's life-support systems remained in good
shape. Most of the bad news came from the Surface Projects manager, who reported a rash of seal failures, maintenance calls, and
diminished redundancy, particularly from the continental and
deep-sea outposts. (The small arctic station reported only routine
maintenance.) This was potentially troublesome, since the downstations used a daunting variety of exotic materials imported from
home; bringing stores and spares back to capacity would take some
cargo shuffling on the part of the Trusts, never an easy sell. But, all
in all, things could be worse.

He soothed the junior managers with promises, dismissed them
at last and went to his cabin.

Alone.

He hated the social isolation of the IOS, but the answer to that
problem, as always, was discipline. That was the mistake the Trusts
had made more than a century ago, tinkering with the genes of
Kuiper volunteers rather than teaching them the practical arts of
self-discipline.

The wall of his cabin showed a relay view of Isis, blue on black
velvet. He was supremely tired of it. He switched the display to a
neutral white luminescence, keyed to dim as he fell asleep.

His personal scroll chirped, waking him early.

The waiting message was tagged amber, important but not urgent. Degrandpre let it wait while he showered and dressed. Then
he dispatched a small personal tractible to bring breakfast from the
galley.

He took up the scroll reluctantly. The message was return traffic from the Works Trust. Perfunctory regrets on the Macabie Feya
death. Revised launch schedules. Revised cargo inventories, projected six months forward.

And in the tail of the message, a small but lethal sting.

An "observer" had been written into the next personnel rotation. A Personnel and Devices observer, a man named Avrion
Theophilus.

Terrifyingly, the man's rank wasn't specified.

On Earth, a man without a title was either very poor or very
powerful. A peasant or a Family man.

And peasants didn't come to Isis.

FOUR

ZOE CAME TO the common room to witness the burning of Macabie Feya's body.

Tam Hayes had called the downstation staff to Yambuku's common room, which was large enough for Zoe to join the crowd without feeling unduly claustrophobic. Hayes had cleared one wall and converted the surface panel into a screen with a view of the western clearances, where remote tractibles had assembled a bier of native wood for the body to lie on. The effect was like watching through a big picture window. But in fact the common room was at the heart of the sterile core of Yambuku, insulated from Isis by onionskin layers of hot-zone laboratories and tractible bays.

Mac Feya, contaminated beyond rescue, hadn't made it farther into the station than the tractible bay. His body was compromised with Isian organisms beyond number; it had become, in effect, a supremely dangerous piece of biological waste. Elam Mather had used a medical remote to sedate and anesthetize Mac as he died, a grim but thankfully brief process; she had then extracted key tissue samples and processed them into the glove-box array before she returned the body to the clearing.

Zoe didn't look at the body too closely. Mac Feya's bioarmor had been stripped for salvage and he had been draped with a white sheet in an attempt to lend some dignity to his corpse. But the body was obviously deliquescing under the shroud, digested by Isian microorganisms and processed with eerie speed into a syrupy black liquid. Just like a CIBA-37 mouse, Zoe thought. She sat rigidly in her chair and tried not to take this death as an omen. A warning perhaps: The Isian biosphere would not be trifled with. But there was nothing malignant here, no deliberate attack on human life. The problem was not Isis, but humanity. We're fragile, Zoe thought; we evolved in a younger and less competitive biological domain. We're infants here.

When the first probes reached Isis, there had been a keen effort to protect the planet from human contamination. But there was not a Terrestrial organism the Isian biosphere couldn't contain and devour, its immense array of enzymes and poisons quickly corrupting the fragile protein envelopes of Earth-based life. The death of Macabie Feya was simply Isis acting as Isis must.

"The planet doesn't hate you," Theo had once said. "But its intimacies are fatal."

Zoe looked away from the body to the forest canopy beyond the bier. The trees were sinuous, thin-boled, raising their limbs like great green hands. This, after all, was her realm, or soon would be. She had trained most of her life for protracted isolation in the Isian woodlands. If a native species had been named, she could name it; she could even supply tentative binomials for new species within a broad range of genera. But this was not a textbook, a file-stack, or a walkthrough simulation. The reality of it was suddenly overwhelming, even from the cloistered safety of the common room: real breezes shaking the foliage, real shadows eclipsing the forest floor. She had come within a few thin walls of Isis—at last, at last.

And in the midst of death. Real death. The depth of emotion in the room was daunting. Dieter Franklin had lowered his head to disguise tears; Elam Mather was openly weeping, and she wasn't the only one.

Two mysteries, Zoe thought. Isis and grief. Of the two, she understood Isis better. How would she feel if someone close to her had died? But there was no one close to her. There never had been. Only Theo, as severe and aloof as some black-winged bird, her teacher and savior. What if it were Theo's body out there? Would she weep? Zoe had wept often when she was young, especially during her dimly remembered time at the Tehran orphan crèche. From which Theo had saved her. Without Theo . . . well, without Theo, she would be lost.

Free, some traitorous part of her whispered.

The thought was disturbing.

Tam Hayes, tall and somber in his Yambuku fatigues, read a brief but dignified eulogy. Then a young biochemist named Ambrosic, the last Reformed Mormon at Yambuku now that Mac was gone, offered a formal prayer for the dead.

On some hidden cue, the attending tractibles doused the bier with hydrocarbon compounds and ignited it with a jet of flame. An external microphone relayed the sound with horrible fidelity, the whoosh of ignition and the slow crackle of the burning wood.

The heat lofted Macabie Feya's ashes high into the Isian sunlight. Wind carried away the smoke. His phosphates would fertilize the soil, Zoe thought. Season by season, atom by atom, the bios would have the whole of him.

Zoe had been sent to Isis specifically for the deep-immersion project, but until the day she would step out of the station, she was a Yambuku hand and had to find a niche for herself. She was neither a microbiologist nor an engineer, but there was plenty of ordinary scutwork to do—filter changes, cargo inventory, scheduling—and she made herself available for all these duties. And day by day, as the shock of Mac Feya's death eased, she felt herself becoming . . . what? If not a member of the Yambuku family, at least a welcome accessory.

Today, a week since the funeral, Zoe had invested eight hours on cargo inventory, which meant lots of physical labor even with the freight tractibles helping. She took a quiet dinner in the refectory and retired to her cabin. More than anything, she wanted a hot shower and an early bed . . . but she had only just dialed the water temperature when Elam Mather knocked at the door.

Elam was dressed in after-duty clothes—loose buff shorts and blouse—and her smile seemed genuinely friendly. "I've got tomorrow's duty roster. Thought you might want a quick look. Or just to talk. Are you busy?"

Zoe invited her in. Zoe's cabin was small, a bedroll and a desk and one wall with a screen function. Once a month or so, compressed edits of Terrestrial entertainment were fed down the particle-pair link from Earth. Tonight most of the station hands were screening the new *Novosibersk Brevities* in the common room. Zoe had linked her screen to an outside camera and the only show she wanted to see was the sleepy crescent of Isis's moon as it fled across the southern stars.

Elam entered the room as she entered all rooms, brusquely, arms at her sides, tall even by Kuiper standards. "I'm not much for light entertainment," she said. "Guess you're not either."

Zoe wasn't sure how to react. Elam didn't flaunt her rank, but she was one of Yambuku's key people, second only to Tam Hayes himself. Back home, it all would have been clear. Junior managers had deferred to her and she had deferred to her seniors—and everyone deferred to Family. Simple.

Elam dropped the roster sheets on Zoe's desk. "It's a desert around here when the entertainment package comes in."

"They say this one has good dancing."

"Uh-huh. Sounds like you're about as enthusiastic as I am. I'm just an old Kuiper fossil, I guess. Where I come from, dancing is something you do, not something you watch."

Zoe couldn't think of an answer. She didn't dance.

Elam glanced at the active wall screen. Zoe had maxed the resolution, creating the illusion that her cabin had lost one wall and was open to the Isian night. Yambuku's perimeter lights picked out the nearest trees, starkly bright against the velvet-dark forest. "No offense, Zoe, but you're like a ghost sometimes. You're here, but all your attention is out there."

"It's what I'm trained for."

Elam frowned and looked away.

Zoe added, "Did I say something wrong?"

"Excuse me? Oh—no, Zoe. Nothing wrong. Like I say, I'm just an old Kuiper fossil."

"You read my personnel file," Zoe guessed.

"Some of it. Part of the job."

"I know how it must sound. Sole survivor of a clonal pod, designed for Isis duty, lost in an orphan crib for three years, mild aversion to human contact. Freakish, and I guess . . . very *Terrestrial*. But I'm really—"

She began to say, *no different from anyone else.* But that was a lie, wasn't it? Even on Earth, she had stood a little apart. And it was part of her qualification for the job.

"—trying hard to fit in here."

"I know," Elam said. "And I appreciate it. I want to apologize if we've been slow about breaking the ice. Mostly it's what happened to Mac, nothing to do with your history."

Zoe noted the qualifier. *Mostly.* But that was fair. The majority of the scientists at Yambuku were Kuiper-born. The old-time Commonwealth Settlement Ministry had populated the first Kuiper Body settlements with citizens gen-engineered for long isolation and the claustrophobically tight conditions in the water mines. Unfortunately, it had been a faulty sequence-swap. The undetected bug in their altered genome had been unexpected, late-life neurological decay, a congenital nerve-sheath plaque difficult to cure or contain. Of that generation of Kuiper settlers, those who survived the rigors of first settlement had died screaming in inadequate clinical facilities far from Earth. Only a hasty program of sequence-patching had saved their children from the same fate. Most of them.

Kuiper veterans would tell you they feared heavy-handed Terrestrial gene-tinkering aimed at population control, not the process itself. But family history made it a ticklish issue. Zoe was a clonal

birth whose life had been designed and tailored for Trust duty. Her
Kuiper-born colleagues must find that distasteful.

"What I'm saying, Zoe, is that none of that matters much.
Because you're one of us now. You have to be. We're sitting at
the bottom of a hostile biological ocean, and Yambuku is a bathy-
sphere. One leak and it's over for all of us. In that kind of environment, we can't afford anything less than mutual trust."

Zoe nodded. "I understand. I'm doing my best, Elam. But I'm
not . . . good with people."

Elam touched her arm, and Zoe forced herself not to flinch.
The older woman's hand was warm, dry, rough.

"What I'm trying to say is, if you need a friend, I'm here."

"Thank you. And I'm sorry if this sounds rude. I look forward
to working with you. But . . . I don't want a friend."

Elam smiled. "That's okay. I didn't say 'want.' "

The days passed, each day a step closer to her liberation from the
confinement of Yambuku. Outside, a week of rain gave way to
vivid sunshine. The station's device shop processed Zoe's excursion
suit, duplicating its files and testing its capacities, green-lighting its
function inventory item by item. Zoe spent the lag time patiently,
learning the first names of Yambuku's sixteen current residents. Of
these, she was most comfortable with Elam Mather and Tam Hayes,
the device-shop engineers Tia and Kwame and Paul, and the
planetologist Dieter Franklin.

"We're close to a go-ahead on your excursion technology,"
Tam Hayes told her. "The technicians are impressed. We were
told to expect something novel. This is more than novel."

Zoe pushed a cargo cart down the long windowless enclosure of the south quarter. The cart's wheels rattled against the
brushed-steel floor. She tried to imagine how this place must have
looked when the tractibles and Turing constructors were assem-
bling it. A metal catacomb attended by mechanical spiders, steel
and metacarbon panels lofting down from orbit on guided para-
chutes.

Today was mainly sunny and warm, according to Hayes. Not that she could tell from the timeless monotony of this walkway. "Days like this," Hayes said, "we often send the dragonfly remensors out."

Zoe looked up from her work.

Hayes said, "Interested?"

Yes, very much.

"Your file says you can handle this kind of remote. Is that correct?"

Zoe adjusted the headset to fit her skull. "Yes."

"And you know the terrain?"

"From simulations."

"Okay. We'll call this a training jaunt. Just keep me in sight at all times and do as I say."

Yambuku operated its telepresence devices from a console room no larger than Zoe's cabin. She was aware of Tam Hayes in the chair next to hers. In Yambuku's ultraclean environment, odors became more intense. She could smell him—a clean smell, soap and laundered cotton and his own unique scent, like spring hay. And, alas, herself: nervous, eager. She activated the headset and the room fell away from her awareness—though not the scent.

Hayes activated the remote, and two dragonfly remensors rose from a bay at the periphery of the shuttle dock into the still noon air.

The remensors' fragile wings glistened with photoelectric chiton cells, microscopic prisms. Their elongated bodies curled downward for stability as the devices hovered in place.

Zoe, wrapped in the headset and hands on the controls, saw what her remensor saw: Yambuku from a height, and the wooded rift valley infinitely deep and wide beyond it, an unbroken canopy of green dappled with gentle cloud shadows.

Her heart hammered. Another wall had fallen. Between herself and Isis there were many walls, but every day fewer, and soon enough, none; soon enough, only the insensible membrane of her excursion suit. The two realms, her Terrestrial ecology of blood and tissue and the deep Isian biosphere, would come as close to physical contact as technology permitted. She longed to touch her new world, to feel its breezes on her body. The feeling was startling in its intensity.

Tam Hayes spoke. He was sitting beside her at the console, but his voice seemed to ring out of the bright blue sky. "We'll take it slowly at first. Follow as close as you can. If you lose sight of my remensor, use the display target to find me. And don't be afraid to ask questions. Ready, Zoe?"

Stupidly, she nodded. But with his headset on he could see only her dragonfly remensor, a device identical to his own. "Ready," she said belatedly. Her hand trembled on the guide stick. Her remensor quivered responsively in the sunlight.

"Up to three thousand meters first. Give you the long view."

As quickly as that, Hayes' remensor spiraled into a vertical ascent. Zoe promptly guided her own dragonfly upward, not following him slavishly but keeping pace, demonstrating her ability. In the upper left corner of her headset an altitude readout flickered ruby iridescence.

At three thousand meters, they paused. The winds here were stronger, and the dragonfly remensors bobbed like hovering gulls.

"Altitude is the best defense," Hayes said. "Given the cost of these remotes, we prefer to keep them away from insectivores. The greatest danger is from aviants. Any large bird within a kilometer will toggle a heads-up alert, at least here in the open. Down in the canopy, things are trickier. Keep your distance from trees if at all possible, and stay at least five or six meters off the ground. Basically, stay sharp and watch the telltales."

She knew all this. "Where are we going?"

"To the digger colony. Where else?"

"Just like that?"

"Just like that."

Zoe decided she liked this man Tam Hayes.

The dragonfly remensors relayed only audiovisual information. As they moved westward, there was no physical sensation of flight. Zoe remained aware of the pressure of the chair against her buttocks, her solid presence in the remote-sensor chamber. But the images she saw were deep, rich, and stereoscopic. And she could hear clearly what the remensors heard: at this altitude, only a gentle rush of air; lower, perhaps the trickle of water, the cries of animals.

Together, they flew across the glinting ribbon of the Copper River, named by Hayes' predecessor for his Kuiper Clan. Large aviants and small predators had gathered to drink along the sandy shore, where slower waters pooled. She saw a herd of epidonts sunning themselves in the shallows. Beyond the river the forest canopy closed tight once more, seed trees and spore trees undulating like so much green linen toward the foothills of the Copper Mountain range.

"It's all so familiar," Zoe whispered.

"Maybe it seems so." Hayes' voice came from the empty sky beside her. "From this height, it might almost be equatorial Earth. Easy to forget that Isis has a wildly different evolutionary history. Work we've done in the last six months suggests that life here remained unicellular far longer than it did on Earth. In Terrestrial organisms, the cell is a protein factory inside a protein fortress. Isian cells are all that but better defended, more efficient, far more complex. They synthesize a staggering array of organic chemicals and exist in far harsher environments. On the macroscopic level—in multicelled organisms—the functional difference is minor. The complexity is what matters. A carnivore is a carnivore and it relates to herbivores in the obvious way. Get down to the cellular level, the fundamental bios of the planet, and Isis looks a lot more alien. And more dangerous."

Zoe said, "I meant the terrain. I've flown this way in a thousand sims."

"Sims are sims."

"Survey-based sims."

"Even so. It's different, isn't it, when the landscape is alive under you?"

Alive, Zoe thought. Yes, that was the difference. Even the best sims were only a sort of map. This was the territory itself, moving, changing. A passage in an ancient dialogue between life and time.

Hayes escorted her lower. She saw his dragonfly remensor flash ahead of her, jewel-bright in the noon sun. The foothills lay ahead, wooded ridges etched with creeks. As the land rose, the forest changed from water-loving vine and cup plants and barrel trees to the smaller succulents that thrived in the stony upland soil. A dispersed ground cover opened fat emerald petals, like the blades of aloe vera. Zoe recited the Latin cognomens to herself, savoring the sound of them but wishing the Isian forest could have taken its common names from an Isian language, if there had ever been an Isian language. The closest equivalent was the cluck-and-mutter vocalizations of the diggers, and whether these constituted "language" in any meaningful sense was one of the questions Zoe hoped to answer.

The digger colony itself, from the air, was exactly like its sims, a cluster of mud and daub mounds in a trampled clearance. Charred remnants of cook fires pocked the soil. Hayes circled the colony once, then descended in a slow spiral, watching the sky for predators attracted by the diggers' refuse heaps. But the sky was clear. Impulsively, Zoe dropped ahead of him. Hayes didn't rebuke her, and she was careful to stay within his security perimeter.

She wanted to see the diggers.

Only still images had been transmitted down the particle-pair link to Earth. She had seen multiple photographs, and more than that, images from a remote autopsy performed on a digger that had been killed by a predator, the carcass salvaged by tractible and dissected by surgical remensors. Bits of it were still preserved in Yambuku's glove-box array—frozen blue and red tissue samples. Zoe had heard recordings of the diggers' vocalizations and had analyzed them for evidence of internal grammar. (The results were ambiguous at best.) She knew the diggers as well as an outside observer could know them. But she had never seen them in vivo.

Hayes seemed to understand her excitement, her impatience. His dragonfly remensor hovered protectively nearby. "Just not too close, Zoe, and don't ignore your telltales."

The diggers were the most widely distributed vertebrate species on Isis. They were found on both major continents and several of the island chains; their settlements were often complex enough to be detectable from orbit.

They were mound-builders and limestone-excavators. Their technology was crude: flint blades, fire, and spears. Their language—if it was a language—was equally rudimentary. They appeared to communicate by vocalizing, but not often and almost never socially—that is, they signaled, but they didn't converse.

Any deeper study of the diggers had been hampered by Isis's toxic biosphere, by the impossibility of interacting with the diggers except through the intermediary of remensors or tractibles . . . and by the difficulty of knowing what went on inside their deeply tunneled mounds, where they spent a good portion of every day.

Zoe descended past the treetops into a cacophony of birdsong. Flowers like immense blue orchids dangled from the high limbs of the trees, not blossoms but a competing species, a saprophytic parasite, stamenate organs projecting from the blooms like pink fingers dusted with copper-red pollen.

She moved lower still, under the tree canopy and into a shade-dappled space where fern-like plants unfurled from the damp crevices between exposed tree roots. Not too low, Hayes reminded her, because a triraptor or a sun lizard might uncoil from some stump or hole and crush her remensor between its teeth. She hovered in the generous, shadowed space between two huge puzzle trees, wings whirring softly, and turned her attention to the digger colony.

The colony was old, well-established. It harbored nearly one hundred and fifty diggers by the last rough count. The population was supported by stands of fruit-bearing trees to the west, plentiful game, and a clear brook—more nearly a river in the rainy season— running out of the high Coppers. To the west was a meadow of sunny scrubweed where the diggers concentrated their excretions and buried their dead. The digger colony itself was a cluster of rock and red-clay mounds, each mound at least fifty meters wide, overgrown with scrub and fungal mycelia.

The digger-holes were narrow and dark, reinforced with a concrete-like substance the diggers made from an amalgam of clay or chalk and their own liquid wastes.

Two diggers were present in the clearing around the mounds, hunched over their work like bleached white pill bugs. One tended the communal fire, feeding windfall and dried leaves into the flames. The other scraped a point onto a length of wood, a spear, turning it at intervals over the fire. Their motion was laconic. Zoe wondered if they were bored. Flints and knapping rocks littered the hardpack soil.

"They're not," Hayes said, "beautiful animals."

She had forgotten that he was beside her. She started at the sound of his voice: too close, too intimate. Her dragonfly remensor wobbled in the shade.

One of the diggers looked up briefly, black eyes swiveling. It was at least fifteen meters away.

"They are, though," Zoe whispered (but why whisper?). "Beautiful, I mean. Not in some abstract way. Beautifully *functional*, beautifully adapted for what they do."

"That's one way of looking at it."

She shrugged, another wasted gesture. The diggers *were* beautiful, and Zoe didn't particularly care whether Hayes could see that or not.

A harsher, stronger evolution had shaped them. One of the diggers stood erect in the sunlight, and she appreciated the versatility Isis had built into it, a sort of living Swiss Army knife. Upright, the digger was a meter and a half tall. Its domed gray head projected from a sheath of flesh like a turtle's head. Its eyes, black and immensely sensitive, rolled in rotary sockets. Its upper arms, the digging arms with their spade-shaped dactyls, hung laxly from high shoulder joints. One of its smaller manipulative arms grasped the new spear, multijointed thumbs wrapped around the wood. Its cartilaginous belly-plates expanded and contracted as it moved, giving it the look of something too flexible for its size, like a giant millipede.

The digger's beak-shaped muzzle opened. It emitted a series of muted clicks, which its companion ignored. Talking to itself?

"That's Old Man," Hayes informed her.

"Pardon me?"

"The digger with the spear. We call him Old Man."

"You named the diggers?"

"A few of the most recognizable. 'Old Man' because of the whiskers. Long white curb-feelers. Everybody at Yambuku's been here by remensor, most of us more than once, and Old Man pays us a return visit from time to time."

"He comes to the station?" Why hadn't this been in the reports? Degrandpre's information triage, she supposed; zoological data sacrificed to production statistics.

"Every few days, 'long about dusk, he skulks around the perimeter of the station, checks us out. Stares at the tractibles if we have any running."

"Then they're curious about us."

"Well, this one is. Maybe. Or maybe we're just an obstacle on the way to his favorite fishing hole. You don't want to jump to conclusions based on one individual's behavior."

Zoe flew her dragonfly remensor in a ragged circle, trying to attract the digger's attention again. Old Man swiveled his eyes toward her instantly.

The sense of *being seen* was almost frightening. In her chair in the remensor cabin, Zoe shivered.

"Speaking of dusk," Hayes said, "the nocturnal insectivores start hunting as soon as the shadows get long. We should head for home soon."

But that's where I am, Zoe thought. I am home.

FIVE

THEY CALLED HAYES "the monk of Yambuku"—partly because he had been on Isis longer than almost anyone else, partly because his work kept him continuously busy. He was diligent about management chores but essentially thought of them as a distraction. What he relished were the rare moments—such as this one—when he found himself back in the lab, with no pressing concern beyond the microanatomy of Isian cells.

What life had achieved on Isis, it had achieved with DNA. Like Terrestrial life, Isian organisms used these long-chain molecules to store and alter hereditary information. But DNA was an encodable molecule, a blank book, and in these similar books, Earth and Isis had recorded very different histories.

There was no evidence of broad mass extinctions on Isis. Early in its history, the Isian stellar system had been as violent as the environment around any young star; cometary impacts had given Isis its water and organic molecules. But some later event, or perhaps the simple presence of an enormous gas giant twice the size

of Jupiter in the outer system, had swept away a great deal of aboriginal rock and ice, at least as far out as the Isis system's icy ring,
its own Kuiper Belt. Life had emerged on a world far more placid
than the primitive Earth.

Life on Isis was a longer, deeper river. Its narrative was slow
and complexly exfoliated, punctuated not by ice ages or cometary
impacts but by waves of predation and parasitism. The Isian ecology
was an evolving, armed detente. Its weapons were formidable, its
defenses ingenious.

Which made the planet, among other things, a vast new *pharmacopeia*. Much of the cost of maintaining Yambuku was paid for
by Terrestrial pharmaceutical collectives under the Works Trust.
And that was a problem, too. Everything that came out of Yambuku had to be justified to Trust accountants. There was no room
here for pure science, as the Kuiper-born employees were made
distinctly aware. Hayes supposed the Trusts specifically liked him
because he hadn't rotated back home and immediately published a
score of articles in the independent academic journals. Giving
away—as the Trusts saw it—what they had paid for.

He finished the work he was doing, microdissecting a bacterial
entity that had been growing on the exterior seals, stored his results
and tidied up the glove box for the afternoon shift.

He looked up as Elam entered the lab. By now, he had learned
to recognize her footsteps. Yambuku had a staff of sixteen, most of
them on yearly rotation, though some, chiefly himself and Elam
Mather, had lived at Yambuku for most of five years now. Kuiper
folk endured such close quarters far more easily than Terrans or
Martians, which meant that most of the Yambuku hands were
Kuiper-born—although they came to Isis strictly as employees of
the Trusts.

"Fresh download from the IOS," Elam said, scroll in hand.
"Do you want to look at it now or later?"

He sighed and gave up his glove-box station to Tonya Cooper,
a resident microbiologist who had been standing at a bench and
tapping her foot impatiently. "We can do this over lunch, I hope?"

"Don't see why not."

. . .

Elam brought her scroll to the lunchroom but set it aside while they ate. Food at Yambuku consisted of uninspiring nutrient chunks of various kinds, assembled from the subgrade output of the IOS's gardens. "Compressed protein," Elam called it, or less kindly, "compost."

"We need to find a more inert substance for the seals," he said.

"Is that possible?"

He shrugged. "Ask the engineers. As it is, we're spending more time on maintenance than on basic research. And running unnecessary risks."

Risking lives, he thought. Yambuku seemed eerily quiet without Mac's roaring voice.

Elam picked up the agenda and spread it out on the tabletop. Hayes scooted his chair closer.

"Item one," Elam said. "Zoe's excursion suit is ready for the walkaround test, according to Tia and Kwame. Zoe, of course, can't wait to take it out. What *we* want is a closely observed walk around the clearances, accompanied by a partner in conventional armor and with heavy tractible support."

"And what Zoe wants is to roam around the forest until she feels like coming back."

"You guessed."

He smiled. "I can talk her out of the long hike. And I'll partner her for the excursion."

"Uh-huh." Elam gave him a speculative look.

"What does that mean—'uh-huh'?"

"How much do you know about our Zoe?"

"The basics. She's clonal stock from the old genome collection, raised by Devices and Personnel."

"She *is* a device, the way they see it. Put it together, Tam. Think of it from the Trust's point of view. They don't give a shit about the linguistic nuances of the diggers or the taxonomics of Isian flora. She's here for some other reason."

He didn't share her fascination with Terrestrial politics. "Devices and Personnel doing another little dance with the Works Trust?"

"More than that, I suspect. The two factions have always been rivals, but Devices and Personnel has been in eclipse since the turn of the century. I suspect they see Isis as their chance to steal a march on the Works bureaucracy. If Zoe's excursion technology performs as promised, it's practically a revolution—we can expand the human presence on Isis way beyond what it is now."

"Elam, we can't even keep our external seals clean."

"And that's the point. Zoe's device isn't just a new technology, it's a dozen new technologies—high-efficiency osmotic filters, stress-resistant thin-film polymers more biologically inert than anything we have . . . it's a coup d'état."

"High praise."

"No, I mean *literally*. The Works Trust has been foundering on Isis for two decades, and the problems only get worse. If Devices and Personnel can step in and make Isis a paying proposition in one swift stroke, they might garner enough Council support to oust the WT hardliners."

All this left Hayes feeling impatient and uncomfortable. "Earth politics, Elam. What does it mean to us?"

"If it works, it means we get a whole new crop of kachos with new priorities. Best case. In the long run, it might mean permanent settlements. It might mean Isis gets rapidly strip-mined for its biological and genetic resources. It would almost certainly mean a lot less Kuiper involvement."

"Would it?"

"Well, why are we here? Partly because the Works people can exploit our scientific savvy without being beholden to Devices and Personnel. Partly because we're accustomed to living and working in small groups in enclosed environments. If Devices and Personnel is prepared to open up Isis to anyone with one of their environmental interfaces—and if they can do that without a humiliating liaison with the Kuiper Republics—then they blow the Works Trust out of the water. And us besides. Not to mention the future of genuine science on this planet. They won't disseminate knowledge, they'll *patent* everything they learn. And bypass us on the way to the stars."

"You suppose Zoe is aware of all this?"

"Zoe is a cat's-paw. She thinks it's all an exozoology project. But Devices and Personnel owns her. Read her file again—the fine print. She was decanted and raised in a high-class D and P crèche until the age of twelve. Then, suddenly, she was dumped into a Tehran orphan ranch along with four clonal siblings."

"A lot of people get shunted off-line like that. Bureaucracy."

"Yeah. But check the date. August of thirty-two—the Works Trust has half the high staff of D and P arrested for sedition. A power struggle. September of thirty-two, Zoe and sibs are dumped in Tehran. January of thirty-five—another staff shake-up, this time in the Works Trust itself. A bunch of Devices and Personnel kachos are reinstated, hauled back from the rehab farms and declared heroes. March, of thirty-five, D and P collects Zoe from the orphan farm."

"Just Zoe?"

"Her sibs didn't survive. Iranian orphan farms aren't exactly the Lunar Hilton. All Zoe knows is that she was rescued. They bought her loyalty, cheap."

"Cheap for them. It must have been traumatic for her."

"Can't you tell?"

He nodded. "She's not exactly well-socialized."

"She's a victim and a tool, raised on promises and theory and thymostats and bullshit. Some advice? Don't get attached."

I'm not attached, Hayes thought. To anything. "She's a long way from home, Elam."

"Not as far as you might think. She has a keeper, a Devices and Personnel kacho named Avrion Theophilus. He was her trainer, her teacher, and her surrogate father after Tehran. And according to this agenda, he's coming to Isis."

Night fell, reflected on a dozen screens throughout Yambuku. Hayes had a session with Dieter Franklin. The tall planetologist drank too much coffee and took his pet theories, something about the microtubule structure of Isian microcells, out for a walk. It was interesting, but not interesting enough to keep Hayes up past midnight.

The station was quieter after dark. Curious, Hayes thought, how we all pace ourselves to these circadian rhythms, even though the Isian day-clock ran a couple of hours slow. He walked the corridors of the core once around, a caretaker's gesture, then went to bed.

Zoe was excited over her first walkabout. She was restrained during the suit-up, but Hayes knew by the color in her cheeks and the flash in her eyes that she had imagined this moment for years.

The memory of Mac Feya rose up to dim his own excitement. Zoe's excursion suit was impossibly flimsy. Elam was right: this wasn't an improved bioarmor, it was a whole catalog of new technologies . . . carefully hoarded, he supposed, by the gnomes of Devices and Personnel. And yes, if it worked, it would transform the human presence on Isis.

Zoe was ready and waiting by the time he had sealed himself into his infinitely more cumbersome bioarmor. She appeared limber and free by comparison, with nothing riding her body but a semitransparent membrane, a pelvic sheath to recycle wastes, a breathing apparatus that hugged her mouth, and a pair of substantial boots.

Elam Mather, supervising from well within the sterile core, reviewed their telemetry and cleared them to leave the station. They had already advanced through three layers of semi-hot exterior-ring cladding; now the final door, a tall steel atmosphere lock, slid open on naked daylight.

Not sunlight. A solid overcast hid the sun and made the nearby forest shadowy and forbidding. Zoe stepped past Hayes in his massive armor and stood in the clearing, looking ridiculously vulnerable. She looked, in fact, almost naked. Her excursion suit gave her features a ruddy glow but concealed nothing.

Her arms and shoulders moved without restraint. Her upper body was supple, small taut muscles moving under blemishless skin. Her breasts were compact and firm. Hayes feared for her, but Zoe was fearless. She moved awkwardly at first, the leg and pelvic gear hampering her stride, but with a coltish, obvious joy.

"Slowly, Zoe," he warned her. "This is a telemetry exercise, not a picnic."

She came to a stop, hands out, chin uplifted. "Tam! Do you feel it?"

"Feel what?"

She was practically giddy. "The rain!"

The rain had begun imperceptibly—at least to Hayes—a gentle mist rolling out of the west. Raindrops spattered the dry clearance and rattled the leaves of the forest. Droplets began to bead on Zoe's second skin. Dewdrops. Jewel-like. Toxic.

Hayes had never been to Earth. The biotic barrier was simply too steep; it would have meant countless inoculations and immune-system tweaks, not to mention a grueling whole-body decon when he moved back into Kuiper space. But he was a human being, and a billion years of planetary evolution had been written into his body. He understood Zoe's pleasure. Warm rain on human skin: What was it like? Not like a shower in the scrub room, he thought—judging by Zoe's helpless grin.

She turned and moved precipitously toward the wooded perimeter, arms loose at her sides. Vine trees looped bay-green leaves above her head. In the wet shade, she was almost invisible. Hayes watched in consternation as she leaned down and plucked a vivid orange puffball from the mossy duff of the forest floor. The fungus dusted the air with spores.

The danger was glaringly self-evident. A single one of those spores could kill her in a matter of hours. A cloud of them wreathed Zoe's head, and she laughed through the respirator with childish delight.

He walked to her, as fast as his armor would permit. "Zoe! Enough of that. You'll overload the decon chamber."

"It's alive," she marveled. "All of it! I can *feel* it! It's as alive as we are!"

"I'd kind of like to keep it that way, Zoe."

She grinned, and silver rain pooled at her feet.

He coaxed her in at last, after a half-hour's stroll around the station perimeter. Back inside, Zoe had finished showering by the time Hayes finally struggled out of his armor. He joined her in the quarantine chamber. Decontamination was agonizingly thorough and there was no sign that the excursion gear had worked less than perfectly, but Yambuku protocols called for a day in isolation while nanobacters monitored both of them for infection.

Two bunks, a wall monitor, and a food-and-water dispenser: That was Quarantine. Zoe stretched out on one of the cots, reduced by these blank walls to something less glorious than she had been in the open air. Hayes filed a brief written report for the IOS's archives, then ordered up a coffee.

Zoe occupied herself by leafing through the six-month itinerary, the document Elam had already shown him. Hayes found himself trying to imagine Zoe as Elam had described her, as a D&P bottle baby lost for two years in some barbaric orphan factory, sole survivor of her brood group.

Nothing quite so dramatic had happened to him, but he understood well enough the emotional consequences of exile and loneliness. Hayes had been born into the Red Thorn Clan, hardcore Kuiper Belt republicans one and all. Red Thorn bred a lot of Kuiper scientists, but he was the only one on the Isis Project—one of the very few Red Thorns on any kind of Trust-sponsored effort. A lot of Red Thorns had died in the Succession, and the clan's opinion of the Trusts was roughly equivalent to a quail's opinion of the snake that devours its eggs.

When Hayes signed his Isis contract, he had been disowned by both clan and family. He was tired by then of Red Thorn extrem-

ism and would not have minded the excommunication, save that
it included his mother—herself an Ice Walker, married to his father
after a Kuiper potlatch in '26. Ice Walkers were equally hostile to
the Trusts but were reputed to value family above all else. When
his mother turned her back on him at the docks, she had been
trembling with shame. He remembered the coral-blue jumper she
had worn, possibly the soberest of all her bright-colored dresses.
He had understood then that he might never see her again, that
this humiliating operetta might be their last living contact.

After that, putting his signature to a Family loyalty oath had
seemed an act as degrading as wading through excrement.

But it was the only road to Isis.

How much worse, though, for Zoe, raised as a machine and
brutalized when D&P fell out of favor. She had taken a loyalty
oath, too, Hayes thought, but hers had been written in blood.

She turned the last page of the itinerary. He saw her mouth
congeal into a frown. "Bad news?"

She looked up. "What? Oh—no! Not at all. Good news!
Theo's coming to visit."

Avrion Theophilus. Her teacher, Hayes thought. Her father.
Her keeper.

SIX

T O A PREVIOUSLY Earth-bound oceanologist such as Freeman Li, the Isian seafloor was a combination of the familiar
and the bizarre in unpredictable proportions.

He would have recognized, perhaps on any similar planet, the
pillowstone lava flows and the active volcanic vents—"black smok-
ers" feeding the deep water with bursts of heat and blooms of exotic
minerals. The powerful light of his benthic remensor picked out
rainbow growths of bacterial mat on the surrounding seafloor, thermophyllic unicells in a thousand variations, almost as ancient as Isis
herself. And this, too, was familiar. He had seen such things in the
deep Pacific, years ago.

Away from these landmarks, the Isian ocean floor was powerfully strange. Highly calciferous plants rose in towers and obelisks
and structures that resembled mosques. Swimming or moving
among them were forms both vertebrate and invertebrate, some of
them large but most very small, shining silvery or pastel-pale under
the unaccustomed light.

Interesting as these creatures might be, it was the simple mono-cells Li had come to collect. Something in these most ancient forms of Isian life might provide a clue to the big questions: how life had evolved on Isis, and why, in all its eons-long exfoliation, that life had not produced anything that could reliably be called sentience.

Behind this lurked the larger question, the question Li had chewed over so often with the Yambuku planetologist Dieter Franklin, the question so central and so perplexing that it began to seem unanswerable: Are we alone?

Life was hardly a novelty in the universe. Isis was testament to that, and so were the even dozen biologically active worlds that had been detected by planetary interferometer. Life was, if not inevitable, at least relatively common in the galaxy.

But there had not been, for all of mankind's attentive listening, any intelligible signal, any evidence of nonhuman space travel, any hint of a star-spanning civilization. We expand into a void, Li thought. We call out, but no one answers.

We are unique.

He stowed his cargo of bacterial scrapings in the remensor's hold and turned back to the surface. He had other work to do. He was the Oceanic Station's chief manager, and this excursion by telepresence had been a guilty pleasure. There were reports to be filed, complaints to be heard. All the dreary business of a Works Trust enterprise to be hacked away like an infestation of barnacles, until it inevitably grew back.

The remensor rose like a steel bubble toward the surface. He watched the seafloor drop away but felt no sensation of motion, only his own stiff spine pressing the back of the chair in the tele-presence room. Running the remensor was so absorbing that he tended to forget to shift position; he always left these expeditions with his chronic lumbar pains acting up.

He reached the point at which daylight became perceptible, the waters around him turning indigo, then sunset-blue, then tur-bulent green. The floating Oceanic Station was in sight, a distant chain of pods and anchors like a string of pearls dangling from the hand of the sea, when the alarm began to sound.

.   .   .

Li handed over the remensor controls to his assistant, Kay Feinn, and scanned the situation report flashing on the remensor room's main screen before he attended to his own rapidly flashing scroll.

General shutdown, barriers up, contamination detected in Pod Six. The lowermost of the Oceanic Station's laboratory units had gone hot. It took him another ten minutes trolling for information before the engineering crew determined that yes, the pod had apparently gone hot, and no, the two men trapped inside it at the time of the alarm weren't responding to repeated calls. Telemetry from the affected pod had also failed; the structure was closed and blank. The electronic failures were particularly perplexing. Faced with locked doors and no input, the engineering people weren't sure what the next step ought to be.

Li knew what it ought to be: He ordered the station's shuttle prepped for emergency evacuation in case of further problems. He told his comms crew to alert the IOS and ask for its advice. He was trying to put through a personal call to Kenyon Degrandpre when Kay, still wearing the telepresence gear, said, "I think you should look at this."

"Not a good time." Obviously.

"I'm down at Pod Six," Kay said. "Look."

He canceled the call and climbed back into the telepresence chair.

Pod Six had been disastrously compromised—that much was obvious from the alarm sequence—but Li couldn't see any physical damage from the perspective of the submersible remensor.

Multiple beams of light thatched the ridges of Pod Six's external sensor array, revealing nothing. Huge translucent invertebrates—Freeman's staff called them "church bells"—drifted toward the remensor in great numbers, attracted by the light; but they were a harmless nuisance, mindlessly trawling the warm equatorial water for organelles. A flock of church bells could hardly have shut down an entire laboratory.

"Kay, what am I supposed to see?"

The two men trapped in the compromised pod were Kyle Singh, a Kuiper microbiologist, and Roe Devereaux, a Terrestrial marine biologist. Even if they had survived the initial biohazard, whatever it was, they might not survive the electrical failure. Even in Isis's warm equatorial seas, Pod Six was deep enough to shed heat quickly. And the air recyclers would already have been overloaded, revved by the alarm protocols into toxic-emergency mode.

But almost certainly, Freeman thought, the men inside were dead by now. Pod Six was home to the deep-sea alkaloid inventory. Lots of hot organisms were down there, and if something had gotten out of the glove boxes and into their air supply, Devereaux and Singh would have toxed out almost immediately. Below Six, there was only the anchor line and the blind deeps of the Isian sea. The water here glowed an inky turquoise, circulating in a thermopause between the habitat of the pressure-loving church bells and the busy phytochemistry of the shallows. Plankton-like monocells and snowflake colonies of bacteria sifted down from the surface waters, a blizzard feeding the biologically rich benthic zones.

The pod seemed intact, if dark. Devereaux had been complaining of algal films clouding the pod windows and external arrays. But none of that was visible to Freeman.

"Circle right," Kay said emotionlessly. "I thought I saw some outgassing at a window seal. Maybe we should get an engineer in here."

He played the remensor's narrow beams across a porthole-like circle of augmented glass.

There. Motion. In the lamplight, a string of rising pearls. Bubbles. Air.

Li's stomach contracted with a more personal fear. This wasn't an overpressure vent or a ballast exchange. Kay was right. This was a leak.

He handed back the remensor gear, called the ops room, and

told the crisis manager to have his men stand by the decouplers. "And keep the ballast detail alert in case we destabilize." A fully breached Pod Six would have to be cut loose or it would drag down the rest of the pods with it. It was a worst-case scenario: Drop the breached pod, hope the tube seals held, and try to keep the whole chain from going pendulum.

Then he took back the telepresence chair and moved the remensor away from the crippled pod, catching a second trail of air in the columns of his lights. More leaks; God, he thought, the lab was a fucking sieve!

And found himself watching with numb panic as the pod began to collapse on itself—quickly and utterly silently. Bimetallic seams geysered froth, then twisted inward, hemispheres of steel torn into ragged blades. There was no sound—his remensor wasn't equipped for it—but the shock must have been tremendous; the remensor bounced hard before it steadied, images ghosting and fragmenting in Freeman's vision. A tremor traveled up the pod chain and rattled the floor under him.

He ordered an emergency disconnect and watched it happen. Explosive bolts severed the pod from the rest of the station. Fragments of debris—polyester cushions, glove-box lattices, aggregates of clothing that might or might not have contained bodies—separated from tangled metal and churned toward the surface. The bulk of the pod simply sank, caught in its own anchor chains, as if a vast hand had reached up to claim it.

Church bells, faintly iridescent, darted through the roiling water and fled into the deeps.

Kenyon Degrandpre hailed a transit tractible to the orbital station's ops room as soon as news of the disaster reached him. He was afraid of what he might learn, but he mustn't let that cloud his judgment. Deal with events now; leave consequences for later.

He found the operations center crowded with junior managers competing for console space. He sent away everyone of less than command status except for the engineers and told the communications crew to stay at their posts pending further orders. Better to have them begging for bathroom breaks than getting underfoot. He kept four subordinates with him and ordered the main screen cleared of everything but traffic from the damaged oceanic outpost.

Where everyone must be very busy. Only the standard telemetry channels were active. Even there, the damage was obvious. The deepest section of the undersea pod chain had imploded only minutes after a biohazard alarm shut it down. Obviously the two events were related, but how? With the pod itself lost, answers might be hard to come by. Not that anyone was looking very hard for answers; the outpost was working frantically to restore its own stability now that it had jettisoned the damaged lab. Degrandpre wondered whether the jettison had been truly necessary or whether Freeman Li might be covering something up, but his engineers assured him it was an act of self-preservation. Still. . . .

But the most immediate question was whether the biohazard had been successfully contained—or whether it might spread.

Degrandpre ordered coffee for all hands in the ops room, then waited with unconcealed impatience for Li—a Terrestrial, at least— to find time for a direct uplink.

Waiting, he felt impotent. This would enrage his superiors on Earth, no matter what happened next. He would have to red-flag a report to the Families and accept whatever responsibility he couldn't dodge. And in the meantime—

In the meantime, he could only pray that the event would be contained.

A junior brought him coffee. The coffee was synthetic and tasted like ashes steeped in well water, but he had drained two cups by the time Li appeared on the screen at last, his Trust uniform disheveled and perspiration-stained. Li's skin was as classically dark as Degrandpre's was classically pale; both men would have been considered moderately handsome on Earth, though not in the Kuiper settlements, where a sort of *muwallad* brown was the fashionable skin color.

Li said without preamble, "I want a full evacuation of the Oceanic Station."

Degrandpre blinked. "You know you don't have the authority—"

"Manager, I'm sorry, but time is important. Whatever it was that took out Pod Six, it affected the men first, the electrical systems second, and then the structural integrity of the pod itself—all in less than an hour. I don't want to lose any more staff."

"According to our telemetry, the problem was contained. If you have any evidence to the contrary, please share it with me."

"With all due respect, I don't have evidence of anything! All I know for certain is that one of my laboratories is at the bottom of the ocean and two of my men are dead. At the time of the accident, they had bacterial plaques in their glove box. I don't know if that contributed to the problem or not, but we have similar organisms in just about every glove box in the station. If it constitutes a threat—"

"You can't know that."

"No, I can't, which is precisely why—"

"You're suggesting we abandon an extremely valuable resource because of one accident and your own surmise."

"We can always reoccupy the station."

"At an enormous expense in resources and work hours."

"Manager . . . *do you really want to assume that risk?*"

The bastard was trying to protect himself in case of more trouble. Degrandpre imagined Li testifying at a Trust inquiry: *Although I requested an evacuation in unequivocal terms. . . .*

"Just give me any hard information you happen to have, Dr. Li, and we'll proceed from there."

Li bit his lip but knew better than to argue. "If you've been monitoring our telemetry, you know as much as I do. The pod went bad this morning. No communication from the crew, only the hazard siren. I ordered the bulkheads sealed. The pod's electrical and life-support systems shut down shortly thereafter, for reasons unknown. An hour after that, the pod lost hull integrity and collapsed under pressure. That's all we know."

"Have you recovered any of the wreckage?"

"We don't have enough tractibles or excursion gear to recover solid wreckage."

"All right. Make the shuttle bay ready for evacuation, but wait for my order. In the meantime, try to gather at least some portion of any evidence that happens to be floating on the surface. Don't bring anything substantial past quarantine, but archive samples for the glove boxes."

"For the record, I strongly recommend evacuating the station now and conducting any investigation by remote."

"Noted. Thank you for your opinion. Please do as I say."

He gave the com control to a subordinate.

When the initial report had been filed and the cleanup delegated—and in the absence of further alarms—Degrandpre put his assistant in charge and issued orders to alert him if the situation deteriorated.

By the clock, he hadn't eaten for nearly ten hours—nor, in deference, had anyone else in the ops room. He ordered a shift change and meals by tractible for anyone staying on duty.

Then he walked to the command commissary, where he found Corbus Nefford dining calmly on braised peppers and basmati rice. The gardens grew a limited range of spices and the IOS biosynthesized others, but Nefford's dish smelled strikingly of fresh garlic and basil.

The physician regarded him with undisguised pleasure. "Join me, Manager?"

Weary, Degrandpre found a chair opposite Nefford. "I assume you've heard."

"About the incident at the Oceanic Station? A little."

"Because I would prefer not to talk about it."

"The crisis is over?"

"Yes." Was that wishful thinking? "The crisis is over."

"Two lives lost?"

"You're as well-informed as I am, apparently. Now talk about something else, Corbus, or be quiet and let me eat." The service tractible waited for his order. He was hungry but he asked for something light—a salad with protein strips.

The chastened physician was briefly silent before a new subject came to mind: "There are fresh Turing gens from Earth, I hear."

"You're a font of good news. I didn't know you took an interest in engineering."

"Only as it affects my future, Manager. Possibly even yours."

"New Turing gens? I don't remember agreeing to a gen switch . . . or are these next year's algorithms?"

"Brand-new gens, apparently, but Engineering tells me they came with a priority tag."

"We're having a hard enough time meeting maintenance schedules as it is. We'll have to modify our quotas, unless this is an efficiency fix."

"Devices and Personnel wants our Turing factories manufacturing parts for a planetary interferometer."

"Nonsense. They floated that idea years ago. Oh, it will have to be done eventually . . . a survey of the local stars, possibly even Higgs launches from the Isis system . . . but not in the near future." An Isian interferometer would be able to image worlds undetectable from the Terrestrial system. But all that was theoretical and would likely remain so for a long time. Rapid expansion into the galaxy wasn't a policy of the Works Trust or of the Families. The only voices calling for an increase in the pace of exploration—with all the fiscal sacrifice that would entail—came from dissident elements in Devices and Personnel.

Unless—

Could Devices and Personnel have become powerful enough to order new Turing gens? Would the Works Trust really sit still for that?

He had been away from Earth too long to guess.

"Manager?"

Nefford was almost salivating for a reaction. Degrandpre declined to give him one. "I'm sorry, Corbus. I was thinking of something else."

The physician's features collapsed into disappointment.

"You'll excuse me," Degrandpre said, standing.

"Manager, what about your meal?"

"Have it sent to my quarters."

Eight hours later, there had been no new development in the outpost crisis. Even Freeman Li had begun to calm down, no longer demanding an immediate evac, only pushing for a "contingency plan," not an unreasonable request. Degrandpre agreed to keep the shuttle bays on standby and ordered an immediate investigation, sending the Kuiper woman Elam Mather from Yambuku to the oceanic outpost to oversee the process. She was a competent worker in her own way, and as an outpost scientist, she would have the skills to supervise cleanup and isolation ops.

After a long session spent briefing the section managers, he returned to his cabin to sort through a stack of recent transmissions from Earth. And yes, Corbus Nefford had been correct; here was an order specifying broad new protocols for the Turing factories, shunting valuable raw material into this scheme to build a large-scale imaging interferometer. Devices and Personnel wanted a functioning planetary imager established before the end of the decade, plus a host of secondary probes to identify small asteroids and Kuiper objects that might ultimately serve as Higgs launchers. Madness! But the Works Trust was cooperating and Degrandpre could hardly resist; the loss of the oceanic lab had already stained his record.

There was a time when he might have enjoyed this kind of intrigue. When he thought he was good at it. But the forces at work here were vast, impersonal, Hegelian. He would be crushed, or he would not; the outcome was beyond his control.

Unless—

Buried in the filestack of communiqués he found a secured order to begin Zoe Fisher's fieldwork "with all possible speed." He took it at first for a Devices and Personnel addendum, but it wasn't; it came with a Works seal. He was taken aback: Rushing the Fisher woman's walkabout might well produce another casualty, another stain on Degrandpre's fragile career record.

And a setback for the radicals of Devices and Personnel? Was that what the Works Trust wanted?

This was delicate indeed. The order *looked* innocuous. The only odd thing about it was that it concerned a Devices and Personnel project but lacked the D&P imprimatur. Significant or not?

One thing was certain. The Fisher woman mattered a great deal, to all sorts of people. She was, as his father used to say, a hinge that bears great weight. Her life—or her death—would surely affect his own.

SEVEN

ZOE HURRIED TO the common room as soon as she heard the news. She found most of the Yambuku family already gathered there—grimly huddled together, many of them, while the main plasma screen displayed fragments of telemetry from the oceanic outpost. She had gone to bed early and was asleep when the first news broke; by the time the all-hands alert sounded, Singh and Devereaux were already confirmed dead, their lab crushed and swallowed by the equatorial sea.

Isis had killed them, Hayes would say . . . though Zoe couldn't bring herself to think of the accident in those terms. Isis wasn't the enemy. She believed that fiercely. The enemy was carelessness, or ignorance, or the unexpected.

Singh and Devereaux had both rotated through Yambuku during their orientation. Most of the Yambuku staff had known them. With the exception of the secretive IOS technicians and the upper-echelon kachos, everyone on Isis duty knew everyone else, especially the handful of downstation crew, the surface dwellers.

Yambuku mourned Singh and Devereaux just as the staff of the oceanic labs must have mourned Macabie Feya.

Three deaths in the time I've been here, Zoe thought. We're like soldiers in a battle zone. We watch each other die.

Tonya Cooper had collapsed onto the shoulder of Em Vya, a junior phytochemist. Both wept quietly. Zoe felt a swelling grief of her own; she hadn't met the dead men but she supposed it must have been an awful death, to be crushed under the brutal weight of the ocean—like Macabie Feya, she thought, lost to the lonely immensities of Isis.

Tam Hayes stood silently in the east corner of the room, next to the large global map of Isis. The globe had been one of Mac Feya's spare-time projects, she remembered Elam saying. A work of art, assembled from Yambuku's redundant supplies—a bubble of handblown silicaflow, physical features read from survey maps in the IOS's archives and etched onto the globe's surface by an assembly tractible. The globe was ice-blue and frost-gray, faintly translucent. She watched Hayes spin the bubble in order to locate the oceanic labs, an infinitesimally small speck in the glassy turquoise of the southern equatorial sea. She joined him, following along as he traced a useless path to the nearest substantial land, a chain of volcanic islands appended to the Great Western Continent like a crooked finger, five thousand kilometers away. Zoe felt she could read his thoughts: *in all that strange blue immensity, more death.* . . .

She put her hand on his arm.

The gesture was impulsive, and she didn't realize at first that she had done it. Her shock unfolded slowly. Hayes seemed not to notice, though he looked up when she pulled away.

The sleeve of his shirt had felt warm, as warm as his body.

"We're losing," he said. "My God, Zoe. Gigadollars to bring us here, to keep us here, and we're losing to the planet." Unasked, he returned the touch, put his hand on her shoulder, and Zoe was simultaneously aware of a number of things: the scent of him, the murmur of the room, the midnight whisper of the station's homeostatics. Seen from outside, Yambuku would be a bubble of yellow light in a moonless dark, the forest's vacant rooms and random corridors reaching to the mountains, the sea. "It goes beyond co-incidence. Maybe Dieter's paranoia is justified. The planet's peeling away our defenses, prying us open. Much more of this and they'll shut us down, conduct research by tractible. . . ."

"It was an accident," Zoe managed to say. *Idiotic*, she thought.

"The Trusts don't care. The Families don't care."

But I care, Zoe thought. And so does he, though he doesn't want to say it so baldly.

Elam Mather came across the room dressed in crumpled sleep fatigues, her eyes full of worry and an active scroll in her hand. "More news from the IOS," she said.

Hayes gave her a wary look.

"They're shuttling me out to the sea lab," Elam explained. "To what's left of it. They want me to find out what happened."

The crew drifted out of the common room as it became obvious that the crisis had stabilized. Zoe, alert now and full of caffeine, sat at a conference table, bathed in the wan light of the active wall displays.

She waited until Jon Jiang, the night-shift engineer, gave her a baleful nod and left the room. Truly alone—and feeling almost furtive—she switched the large west-wall display away from its static readout mode to monitor the view from an exterior camera.

Cool outside tonight, according to the status crawl at the top of the display. Twenty-one degrees Celsius, winds from the west-northwest averaging five klicks per hour. Stars glittered like garnets in the heavy sky, obscured by a cirrus haze.

She felt strange. She couldn't name the way she felt.

She was reminded of the way she had felt years ago when Theo had come to save her from the bleak hallways and morbid stone chambers of the Tehran orphan crèche. That contradictory *mixture* of feelings: dread of the future, dread of this tall stranger in his crisp black uniform, and at the same time a nervous elation, a sweet suspicion of freedom.

Her memories of Tehran had been "smoothed"—the medical word—until they were distorted and affectless. She knew only that her jailers had raped and starved her sisters and had used her own body as they pleased. She didn't forgive them, but her rage was muted; most of her tormentors would have died in the riots of '40, in the fire that had swept out of the industrial slums and swallowed the crèche complex. They were dead, and she was alive; better still, she had been given back the special destiny for which she had been born: the stars.

Why, then, did she shiver at every touch of the material world? She had shivered, outside in her excursion suit, at the first cool drop of Isian rain on her shoulder. And she had shivered at the touch of Tam Hayes' broad, rough hand.

I don't like to be touched. How often in her life had she repeated that small mantra? It was a legacy, the medical ontogenists had told her, of the Tehran years. An aversion too deep to root out, and anyway, where she was going, there would be no one to touch her; no one human, at least, during her alone time in the Isian wilderness.

But then why was she looking at the night sky with her eyes full of tears? Why did her hand stray repeatedly to her shoulder where Tam Hayes had touched her, as if to shelter that ghost of his warmth?

Why had memory begun to well out of her like some dark subterranean spring?

She knew only that something was wrong with her. And that she mustn't tell anyone. If they suspected she was ill, they would send her back to the IOS, probably back to Earth.

Away from her work.

Away from Tam Hayes.

Away from her life.

Two days passed. The crisis at the oceanic outpost had been contained; the mood at Yambuku lightened somewhat, though Zoe noticed the biohazard people keeping their scrolls open on their desks, alert for news. She spent a morning doing a simulation walk through the lush terrain west of the Copper River, then took her lunch into the prep room of the docking bay, watching the maintenance crew ready the shuttle for Elam's suborbital flight across the ocean.

Maintenance was an Engineering duty. Lee Reisman, Sharon Carpenter, and Kwame Sen waved at Zoe from the bay, and Kwame in particular stole a number of more frequent glances at her. Was he attracted to her? Sexually attracted? The thought was unsettling. Zoe had studied with peers at the D&P facilities back home, but most of her classmates were heterosexual women or junior male aristocrats sporting orchidectomy badges. And Zoe hadn't cared. The medical team had taught her a broad range of masturbation sutras, because that was expected to be her permanent sexual modality. It should have been enough.

But these days she was masturbating almost nightly, and when she did . . . well, as often as not, she thought of Tam Hayes.

Elam Mather entered the prep room and joined Zoe at the table, pushing aside a stack of checklists to make room for her coffee cup. The older woman nodded at her abstractedly but said nothing, only gazed at the shuttle work. Kwame kept his glances to himself.

Zoe said, "I hope you have a safe trip."

"Hm? Oh. Well, don't wish me luck. It's bad luck, wishing people luck."

It was the sort of bewildering thing Kuiper people were apt to say. Certainly, Zoe had read all the histories; she could recount the founding of the Republics as well as any schoolchild in the system. But none of that dry knowledge had prepared her for the reality of a Kuiper-dominated community like Yambuku—the frightening fluidity of rank, the unabashed sexuality. Kuiper males were never gelded, no matter what their station in life, and the result was rather like being caged with zoo animals; these people made no secret of their urges, their assignations, their copulations. . . .

"We're not so bad," Elam said.

Zoe stared. "Are you telepathic, too?"

Elam laughed. "Hardly. It's just not the first time I've worked with Terrestrials. You learn to recognize that expression, you know, that sort of—'Oh, God, what *next?*' "

Zoe allowed herself a smile.

"Actually," Elam added, "you're adjusting very well for an Earth-bound hand."

"I'm not Earth-bound. Any more than you're Kuiper-bound. I mean . . . we're *here*, aren't we?"

"Good point. You're right. We're here. We're not what we used to be." She returned Zoe's tentative smile. "I begin to understand what Tam sees in you."

Zoe blushed.

Thinking: *He sees something in me?*

She dreamed that night of her first home—not the horrid barracks in Tehran but the soft, cool Devices and Personnel crèche of her baby years.

The crèche was located deep in an American wilderness enclave. The crèche dome, green as crystal, seen from afar on picnic days, had glittered like a dewdrop on the rolling prairie grassland.

The nursery wards and crèche pads had been as plush as velvet, all corners rounded, the air itself sweet-smelling and cool. And she had not known fear or doubt, not in the crèche. Each of the nannies, many of them wholly human, tended one special child, and they were stern but kind, fat ministering angels.

She had changed her green jumper every morning and every afternoon, the simple cloth starched and bright. And she had looked forward to the evening bath, splashing with her sibs while lactating nannies with babies in their arms looked on indulgently from terraces above the steaming water.

In her dream she was back in the bath pool, slapping waves at a yellow flotation ring. But the dream became disturbing when great, ancient trees—cycads or giant lycopods—erupted around the pool, a sudden forest. The voices of her sibs were instantly stilled. She was alone, shivering, naked in a woodland like no woodland she had ever seen. She climbed from the crèche pool onto a mossy shore. Black soil cushioned her feet; the rocks were dressed in velvety green liverwort. She didn't know how she had come here or how to find her way home. She felt panic rising out of the clenched fist of her belly. Then a shade, a shape, appeared out of the humid fog. It was Avrion Theophilus, her own beloved Theo in his crisp Devices and Personnel uniform . . . but when she recognized him she turned away and ran, ran as fast she could run, ran uselessly while his footsteps thudded behind her.

She woke in the dark.

Her heart was hammering. It eased soon enough, but the sense of threat and electricity continued to vibrate through her body.

Just a bad dream, Zoe thought.

But she never had bad dreams.

She pushed the nightmare out of her mind, thinking again of Tam Hayes, of how she had touched him so unselfconsciously in the common room, of the fabric of his shirt, of his eyes holding hers for a fraction of a moment.

Something is wrong with me, she told herself again, oh God, as she reached between her legs and spread her labia with her fingers, finding the bump of her clitoris like a small, hard knot.

The orgasm came quickly, a wave of fire. She bit her lip to keep from crying out.

EIGHT

LAM MATHER FELT her usual light-headedness as the shuttle lifted from Yambuku into a watery sky. Isis fell away beneath her, but not far enough; this was a suborbital flight, half a world's journey to the damaged oceanic outpost. Several hours' flying time at the best speed the cumbersome shuttle could make. Planets, she thought, were simply too large.

The shuttle crew were IOS-based, and most of them were Kuiper-born, pleasant enough but not talkative. Elam settled down in an aisle seat by herself, her scroll tuned to one of the Terrestrial pop-novels occasionally dumped down the particle-pair link for the presumed edification of lonely outposters. This one (titled *E. Quan's Difficult Decision*) was the story of a young girl from a mesomanagerial family, in love with a Family cousin who has mistaken her station in life. Alas, a tragedy. The young heir, on learning that he can't decently marry our heroine, volunteers for an orchidectomy and the girl slinks back to her commune, chastened but wiser.

What crap, Elam thought. In real life, the meeting would never happen; or if it did, there would be no question of a love affair. The aristocrat would fuck the prole and forget her name the next day. Certainly no such well-connected male would ever consent to an orchidectomy. Gelding was a way to keep the salarymen away from High Family daughters, no more and no less. Kachos like Degrandpre were proud of their scars, but that was only because they had been bred to a life of glorified servitude.

The proles, the great unconsulted Terrestrial masses, simply fucked or married as best they could. And increased their numbers, though the various unchecked infertility viruses helped keep the population within limits.

Elam had taken much of her schooling on Earth. She was not naive about the planet . . . unlike Tam Hayes, or even a D&P bottle baby like Zoe Fisher.

She turned to the window, which wasn't a window at all but a direct video feed from a cam on the outside of the multiply-insulated shuttle. The continent fled westward beneath her. Isis looked heartbreakingly calm from this altitude. The snowcapped Copper Mountains had given way to broad alluvial plains, to prairie veined with sky-blue rivers. Clouds scrubbed the grasslands with shadow, and rivers broadened at last into swampy bays and salty inlets, the vast eastern littoral where seabirds wheeled in flocks large enough to be visible even from this altitude. All this more known than seen: mapped from orbit; glimpsed, if at all, from shuttle flights or through the eyes of long-range tractible remensors.

Untouched, all this, Elam thought. In a sense, no part of Isis had ever been touched, certainly not by naked human skin. The planet was full of life, but this was life older than Earth's by a billion years, more evolved but also more primitive, preserved from change by the absence of great waves of extinction, room for all, for all genera and every survival strategy save the human, the sentient, the Terrestrial. We're such simple creatures, she thought; we can't tolerate these finely honed phytotoxins, the countless microscopic predators shaped by a billion years of involution. Nothing in the armory of the human immune system could recognize or repel the invisible Isian armies.

They lay siege to us, Elam mused. She thought of the bacterial colonies eroding the seals at Yambuku and of the algal films that might or might not have contributed to the deep-sea disaster. We don't recognize them, but I do believe they recognize us. We build our walls, our barriers, but life talks to life. Life talks to life; that was the rule.

The gray-blue continental shelf fell away behind the shuttle, and for a time there was only the ocean to see, cobalt-blue, wrinkled with white breakers; or the cloud tops, often turbulent, tropical storms winding up in the stark sunlight like watch springs coiled with lightning. In all the open sea there was no vessel or wake of a vessel, nothing human, not a nailed board or a bleached plastic bottle; nothing down there, she thought, but the alien krill, clumps of saltwater weed, wind-driven foam.

She thought of the barriers between Isian and Terrestrial life, and then of the long quarantine between Earth and the Kuiper Republics, the dark days when Earth had lost so much of her population to the plagues and the Republics became truly independent, almost by default. The Republics were an alliance of the most remote and hostile environments mankind had ever settled—Kuiper bodies, asteroids, Oort mines, the Martian airfarms. The hydrogen/oxygen economies of the outer system had been severed from the smug water-wealth of Earth itself, humanity splitting like a parthenogenic cell, but the division was never absolute; life touches life. The Works Trust had taken a troubled Earth back into space but could not repair the old civil and political wounds. Earth had retreated into a system of bureaucratic aristocracy; the Kuiper Republics were its unruly children, making pagan or puritan utopias of their icy strongholds—nobody cutting off his balls as a gesture of, for God's sake, *fealty*.

And yet, life touches life.

Take Tam Hayes. A true Kuiper orphan, excommunicated by the doctrinaire Red Thorns for signing up with a Works project.

But signing up with the Trusts was the only way to reach Isis, distant Isis, fabled Isis, the Mandalay of the Republic. He had traded his history for a dream. And Zoe Fisher, as obedient a bottle baby as any that Earth had produced. No dreams allowed, not for that female gelding. But Isis had stitched them together somehow. It was obvious to everyone but themselves . . . certainly to Elam. Put them in the same room and Zoe orbited him like a sun; he followed her like a tractible antenna.

Elam didn't approve of Terrestrial/Kuiper liaisons; most of them didn't last . . . but here, she thought, was something Devices and Personnel might not have anticipated, a small wrench in the harsh human machinery of the Trusts.

Life, doing the unexpected.

She approved. *Maybe* she approved. But there were things Tam didn't know about Zoe, things Elam supposed she ought to tell him. She opened her scroll and began a message . . . she could send it after touchdown.

She wrote until her attention was attracted by a string of volcanic islands passing under the right wing, green to the rims of their ancient caldera. Reefs, not of coral but deposited by a wholly different community of limestone-fixing invertebrates, teased the shallow water into multicolored foam. The light was longer here, making valleys of the low swells. Had she slept? A crewman, passing, told her the shuttle was less than half an hour from docking and decon.

She adjusted her seat restraint, tucked her scroll away and closed her eyes again, thinking of Hayes and Zoe, of the tenacity of life, of the universal need to merge, combine, exfoliate . . . and of the vulnerability of life, too, and of the sea, of the large fish that eat the little fish, and of the long reach of the Earth.

The deep-sea station's head kacho was Freeman Li, a Terrestrial whom Elam had worked with both in training and on Isis. She liked him better than she did most Terrans: he was a flexible

thinker, a small barrel-chested dark-skinned man with Sherpa an-
cestry and family in the Martian airfarms. A fuss-and-worry type,
but he usually worried to good effect.

He was worried now. He took Elam directly from decon to
the nearest common room, a low-ceilinged, octagonal chamber
between a microbiology lab and the engineering deck. Elam assumed she was under sea level here, but there was no way of knowing; the oceanic outpost was as tightly sealed as Marburg or
Yambuku were. The station's distributed mass and deep anchoring
prevented it from moving with the swell, though typhoons caused
it to oscillate, or so she had been told, like a slow plumb bob. There
was no motion now.

"I'll be frank with you, Elam," Li said, absently stirring a cup
of black tea. "When this happened, I told Degrandpre I wanted a
complete evacuation. I still think that's what we should have
done—and ought to do. Whatever killed Singh and Devereaux
and destroyed Pod Six acted far too quickly for us to play with it.
And there are still no obvious candidates for causative agent. Lots
of toxic agents down there, but much of that material is also sitting
in glove-box arrays all over the station. Any agent unique to Pod
Six could only have been a chemical isolate or extract, not live
biota."

"Caustic substances?"

"Some of them extremely caustic, yes, and all highly toxic. A
significant release could easily have killed two men and triggered
the biohazard alarm. But the damage to the pod itself, no, no single
agent or combination of agents could conceivably have done that."

"As far as we know."

He shrugged. "You're right. We *don't* know. But we're talking
about chemical isolates at the microgram level."

"Any other problems, prior to the disaster?"

"Pod Six had problems with algal gunk interfering with the
samplers and sensor arrays. But don't jump to conclusions, Elam.
We've had much the same trouble all up and down the station,
though it gets worse with depth. It would be a tremendous coin-
cidence if both things happened simultaneously—a toxic release

inside the pod and a compromised seal serious enough to collapse the structure itself."

"Whatever caused the watertight seals to break down might also have taken out the glove-box array."

"Maybe. Probably. And doesn't that suggest to you a hazard of the first order?"

She thought about it. "All we have that would make Pod Six unique is a heavy algal infestation in the sensor arrays?"

"I don't know about unique. It's a matter of degree. But in the sense you mean, yes."

"Can I look at these organisms?"

"Certainly."

F reeman Li had hedged Degrandpre's bet by confining his staff to the upper two pods of the chain, where they could make a quick escape to the shuttle bay if the need arose. The remaining three pods had been closed and sealed. That cut into station productivity in general and interrupted at least two very promising research lines, but, Li said flatly, "That's Degrandpre's problem, not mine."

It was a laudably Kuiper-like sentiment, Elam thought.

She followed him down a narrow access shaft to the lowermost of the occupied pods. The bulkheads caught her eye as she passed beneath them: immense steel pressure doors ready to snap shut in an unforgiving fraction of a second. In that awful Terrestrial novel, there had been a passage about a mouse walking into a trap. She had never seen a mouse or a mousetrap, but she imagined she knew how the animal felt.

Precautions in the microbiology lab, never less than stringent under Freeman's watch, had been tuned since the accident to a fine pitch. Until further notice, all Isian biota and isolates were to be treated as proven hot Level Five threats. In the lab's secured anteroom, Elam donned the requisite pressurized suit with shoulderpack air and temperature controls. As did Li, and with his headgear in place he looked peculiar: hollow-eyed, somber. He guided her through the preliminary washdown, past similarly dressed men and women working at glove boxes of varying complexity, through yet another airlocked antechamber and into a smaller, unoccupied lab.

Elam felt some of the terror she had first felt on entering a Level Five viral-research lab during her training on Earth. Of course, it had been worse then. She had been a naive Kuiper student raised on Crane Clan tales of the horrors of the Terrestrial plague years. The great divide between Earth and the Kuiper colonies had always been a biological chasm, deeper in its way than the simple distances of space. The Kuiper clans enforced a quarantine: no one was permitted to arrive or return from Earth unless he or she was scrubbed of all Terrestrial disease organisms, down to the cellular level. Terrestrial/Kuiper decon was grueling, physically difficult, and as lengthy as the long loop orbit from the inner system. There had never been an outbreak of Terrestrial disease on an inhabited Kuiper body; had there been, the settlement in question would have been instantly quarantined and decontaminated—hygiene protocols that would have been impractical on Earth, with its dense and mostly impoverished population.

Elam had gone to Earth for her post-doc the way a fastidious social worker might consent to enter a leper colony: squeamishly, but with the best of intentions. She was inoculated for every imaginable microphage, prion, bacteria, or virus; nevertheless, she came down with a classic "fever of unknown origin" that persisted through the first month of her orientation before it finally yielded to a series of leukocyte injections. She had never been sick in her life before that day. Being sick, being infected with some invisible parasite, was . . . well, even worse than she had imagined.

After that, her first attempt at sterile work had terrified her. The University of Madrid was a Devices and Personnel stronghold full of offworld students, mainly Martians but including several Kuiper expats like herself. Novices weren't allowed in the same room with live infectious agents. She had already been introduced to anthrax, HIV, Nelson-Cahill 1 and 2, Leung's Dengue, and the vast array of hemorrhagic retroviruses, but strictly by telepresence. Virus-handling of the kind required by Terrestrial fieldwork was infinitely more dangerous. Here were all the antique horrors of Earth, predators more subtle and tenacious than jungle animals and just as lively, still stalking the malnourished populations of Africa, Asia, Europe. Shepherd's crooks and rainbow-colored protein loops, all brimming with death.

Planetary ecology, she had thought. Ancient and unbelievably hostile. This was Tam's bios made tangible, the involute residue of evolutionary eons.

But at least Earth had accommodated mankind into the equation, for all the deadliness of its plagues. Isis had brokered no such deal.

She watched as Li put his hands into a glove box. No telepresence here, either, barring the devices that translated his hand motions to the manipulators deep in the vault-like specimen barrels. A glove-box microcamera fed images to Li's headgear and to a monitor where Elam could watch his work. The image of a linked group of living cells filled the screen.

"This is the little bastard that's been fouling our externals. Grows in colonies, a slimy blue film. And yes, there was an inert sample from this culture in Pod Six, but I can't believe there's any causal connection. As a matter of fact—"

The image listed like a sinking ship. "Li? You're losing focus."

"This gear is as old as the station. Degrandpre's been sitting on our maintenance requests for more than a year. Afraid he'll offend the budget people, the timid bastard. Hold on. . . . Better?"

Yes, better. Elam peered at the organism on-screen, fighting an urge to hold her breath. The cell was multinucleated, its spiky protein coat notched like a cog in a clockwork. Mitochondrial bodies, more varied and complex than their Terrestrial counterparts, transited between the fat nuclei and the armored cell walls, sparking quick osmotic exchanges. None of the processes were as well understood as the microbiologists liked to pretend. Different bios, different rules.

"Looks like *our* gunk," Elam said.

"Pardon me?"

"Bacterial slimes on the external seals."

"Like this?"

"Well, not exactly. Yours are ocean dwellers, ours are airborne. I don't recognize those granular bodies in the miotic canali. But the way they lock together is awfully familiar. Um, Li, you're losing the image again."

Freeman Li said, uncharacteristically, "Fuck!" His shoulders straightened sharply. There was a pause. The image swam into an unrecognizable meshwork of colored pixels, and this time it didn't resolve.

Then Li said in a brittle tone, "Leave the chamber, Elam."

There was a sudden hissing sound she couldn't identify. Elam felt the first touch of real fear now—a tingle in her jaw, a dull roar in her ears. "Li, what is it?"

He didn't answer. Under his protective gear, he had begun to tremble.

Instantly, her mouth went dry. "God, Li—"

"Get the fuck out of here!"

She moved without thinking. Her lab reflexes weren't fresh but they were deeply ingrained. He hadn't asked her for help; he had issued an order, on the authority of whatever it was he'd seen in the glove box.

She ran for the lab door, but it was already gliding shut, a slab of oiled steel. Ceiling fans roared to life, producing negative pressure and drawing possibly contaminated air up into series of HEPA and nano filters. A siren began to wail through the pod. It sounded, Elam thought madly, like a screaming child. She moved toward the door as the gap narrowed, knowing even as she ran that the margin of time was impossibly thin; she was already, in effect, sealed inside.

She turned, gasping, as the bulkhead slid into place. The pod was airtight now. The fans stopped, though the siren continued to shriek.

Freeman Li had taken his hands away from the glove box. Something had peeled away patches of his suit and gloves, turned the impermeable membranes into scabs of onionskin. Whole sections of raw flesh were exposed and beginning to blister.

So impossibly fast!

He tore off his goggles. His face was a mask of blood, nostrils gushing freely, his eyes already scarlet with burst capillaries.

He said something incomprehensible—it might have been her name—and collapsed to the floor.

Elam's heart raced. She didn't scream, because it seemed to her that the siren was already screaming on her behalf, that all the dread in the world had been summed into that awful noise. The floor of the pod seemed to slip sideways; she sat down hard on her tailbone a scant meter from Freeman Li's twitching corpse.

She put her fingers to her own nose, drew them back and looked blankly at the bright red spots of blood.

So this is death, she thought. All this red mess. So untidy. She closed her eyes.

NINE

THE SPIN OF the IOS was fortuitously timed. Kenyon De-grandpre was at his small office viewport and looking in the right direction when the latest Higgs sphere arrived.

The effect wasn't spectacular. He had seen it before. A flash in the starry sky, that was all, brief as summer lightning: a scatter of photons and energetic particles, and then the afterglow, a blue Cherenkov halo. A Higgs launch tortured the vacuum around itself, forcing virtual particles into unequivocal existence. It was not simply a journey but, in its way, an act of creation.

The Higgs sphere with its carefully shielded cargo was of course invisible at this distance, a speck in the greater darkness, still half a million miles away. Rendezvous tugs had already left the IOS to retrieve it, the sphere's transponder announcing its location and condition. But of course it had arrived exactly where it was expected. Higgs translations were accurate to within a fraction of a kilometer.

The Works Trust had supplied Degrandpre with a cargo manifest; he held it in his hand. Aboard that invisible spacecraft were a number of unfamiliar and ominous things. Radical new genetic algorithms for the Isian Turing factories. Small robotic probes to be launched into the outer system. And, far from least, the new man, the "observer," the cipher, the threat: Avrion Theophilus. Degrandpre's rather dated *Book of the Families* described Theophilus as a high-level Devices and Personnel officer, loosely connected to the Psychology Branch as well as a distant relative of the Quantrills and the Atlanta Somersets. Which might mean . . . well, anything.

Degrandpre turned to his scroll and called up Zoe Fisher's file, scanning it again for clues. Apart from the obvious connection with Theophilus—he had been her case manager—there was no hint of his hidden agenda. Or of hers, assuming that this Zoe Fisher really was some kind of D&P dog-in-the-manger. He couldn't imagine what Terrestrial dispute might turn on the fate of one bottle baby, for all her fine new technology and linguistic skills. But history had often enough turned on smaller fulcrums: a bullet, a microbe, a misplaced word.

Restless, he called Ops for an update on the Turing manifests. What came back through his scroll was the sound of confusion, until Rosa Becker, his second-shift supervisor, picked up a voice link. "Sir, we're having problems with our telemetry."

Degrandpre closed his eyes. God, no. Please. Not now. "What telemetry?"

"Telemetry from the deep-sea outpost. It's gone. We're blank here—the station's just off the map."

"Tell me it's satellite malfunction."

"Only if we lost all our redundancies at once . . ." A pause, another crackle of hurried conversation. "Correction. We have a single shuttle upbound from the pod chain. Reporting survivors on board. But that's all."

"What do you mean, that's *all?*"

"According to the pilot . . ." Another pause. "No other survivors. Just wreckage."

Just wreckage.

Freeman Li's nightmare had come true.

"Sir?"

And mine, Degrandpre thought.

"I want that shuttle quarantined indefinitely," he said, facing the immediate threat, postponing his own fear. "And sound the stations. We're on full alert."

But he felt like a dead man.

The occasion was Zoe's first solo excursion, the final systems test before she attempted a daylong hike to the Copper River. Tam Hayes left his work—gene-mapping the monocell cultures—and crossed the core quad to the north wing, where Zoe was already suiting up.

His thoughts careened between Zoe's excursion and his research. In both cases, mysteries outnumbered certainties. Cellular genetics on Isis would remain a puzzle for years, Hayes was certain. The biochemical machinery was infuriatingly complex. What to make of organelles that also led independent lives outside their parent cells, that reproduced as retroviruses? Or the tiled complexities of microtubules ringing the cell walls? Every question begged a thousand more, most of them concerning Isian paleobiology, a field of study that barely existed. Apart from a couple of glacial core samples and Freeman Li's work with thermophyllic bacteria, there wasn't any hard data, only conjecture. All those unbroken years of evolutionary recomplication had obviously bred ancient parasitisms deep into the mechanism of life—every energy exchange, every selective ionization, every release of ATP was a fossilized act of predation. Complex symbiotic partnerships had arisen the way mountains rise from the clash of tectonic plates. Out of conflict, collaboration; out of chaos, order. The mysteries.

His mother had trained him in the Mysteries, had taken him to chapel every month. Both Red Thorns and Ice Walkers were primarily Old Deists, a faith much given to philosophizing. The monthly sermons had gone over his head, but he thought often of the annual invocation in the observatory chamber. He had been taken into that cold, domed space to count constellations like rosary beads while the warm bodies of the congregation pressed against him, voices joined in hymns as his mother clutched his hand so tightly it hurt. Was it entirely his fault, then, that he had fallen in love with the stars?

The Red Thorns had thought so.

He found Zoe in the prep room struggling into her excursion suit, Tia and Kwame tabbing the seams for her. Kuiper-born, the two had never learned to respect Terrestrial nudity taboos and they obviously didn't know or care why Zoe flinched at their touch. She looked at Hayes with a rescue-me expression.

He sent the two technicians down to the shuttle bay to give Lee Reisman a hand.

"Thank you," Zoe said meekly. "Really, I can do this myself. They designed the gear that way. It just takes time."

"Shall I leave too?"

She thought for a moment, then shook her head.

"If you need help, ask."

She drew on the leggings, the active membrane as limp as plastic film until it found and matched the contours of her skin; then it mapped itself in place, pinkly translucent, a second skin. She bent to pull on the more conventional hip boots, her small breasts bobbing.

She looked up, caught his eye and blushed conspicuously. Hayes wondered if he should turn away. What would a Terrestrial do?

She pulled her arms through the filmy torso membrane and said something too quiet for him to hear. He cleared his throat. "I'm sorry?"

"It would be faster if you sealed the tabs."

He came across the room, recognizing his eagerness to touch her and suppressing it; she was easily frightened. . . . The tabs of the excursion suit were three bars of fleshy material where the seams met across the small of her back. He touched her skin where it dimpled against the curve of her spine and felt an odd sense of familiarity . . . she was practically a Kuiper woman, at least genetically, her genome sampled from the stock that had settled the

asteroids, hardy raw material for a new diaspora. . . . He sealed the
garment gently and watched the membrane form itself to her body,
heard her indrawn breath as the protective skin tightened over
breasts, nipples, the base of her throat. Without the headgear, without the waste-management pack, she might have been naked. His
hand lingered on the ridge of her hip, and she shivered but didn't
object.

But when he raised his hand to touch her hair, she ducked her
head away. Whispered, "Not there."

"Why not?"

"Only where I'm protected."

She wouldn't meet his eyes.

Was this what she wanted? Needed? He put his hands on her
waist and drew her closer. "Protected," she had said: protected
against contact, he supposed, or against the idea of contact.

He wanted to tilt up her head and say something comforting.
He might have, if the station alarm had not sounded.

Zoe gasped and backed away as if stung.

Hayes looked at the blinker on his pocket scroll. Something
about the oceanic outpost. No details, but obviously more bad
news.

It was the bios, Hayes thought, closing in on him again.

PART
TWO

TEN

ZOE WASN'T TRULY alone in the forest. She was surrounded at all times by insect-sized remensors and larger, spider-legged tractibles; and she was linked to Yambuku by extensive telemetry . . . but she *felt* alone, unspeakably alone, especially after midnight.

This was what she had been born for, this aloneness. Her hermetic impulse had been built into her DNA, the same gen mods the first Kuiper colonists had carried into the emptiness beyond Neptune—a race of monks, carving their hermitages out of frozen, starlit massifs. She was not afraid to be alone.

Which didn't mean she wasn't afraid.

She found herself frightened of a number of things.

She woke well after midnight in the darkness of her tent. The tent was a simple polymer-and-foam geodesic, designed not to protect her from the elements—her excursion suit did that—but to disguise her from the native wildlife. The excursion suit was a semiopen system; she carried food and water in sterile containers with

self-sealing nozzles, but she excreted the inevitable wastes—
bluntly, piss, shit, and CO_2. Her wastes were scrubbed by the suit's
processors and nanobacters, but even sterilized human waste was a
magnet for Isian predators. Solid and liquid wastes could be contained and buried, but her breath and perspiration were harder to
conceal. The tent helped, circulating external air slowly and bleeding her molecular signature through osmotic and HEPA filters.

But no system was perfect. The loss of the Ocean Station less
than ten days ago had made that perfectly clear. Systems were im-
perfect, or imperfectly adapted to the Isian biosphere, which led to
the unhappy thought that she might even now be attracting nocturnal predators that had evaded her perimeter defenses.

That hushed, woody rattle in the distance, for example, might
be wind in the trees, or it might be. . . .

Bullshit.

She sat up, exasperated, all hope of sleep fled. She found it hard
enough to rest in the excursion suit, which faithfully reported to her
skin the pressure of every twig and pebble under the gel floor of the
tent—but it was worse to be afflicted with the midnight jitters. An array of robotic remensors scanned her perimeter at all times for motion
or telltale molecular signatures; nothing larger than a grub could sneak
up on her. And her tent was, if not perfect, certainly grub-proof.

So to hell with nagging fears. She was just restless. She pulled
on her protective leggings, opened the tent door and stepped out
into the windy darkness of the cycad-like Isian forest.

The only ambient light came from a sprinkle of stars above the
leaf canopy, but there was enough of it to give the suit's photon
multiplier something to work with. The forest through her iris
lenses appeared as a map of squat tree boles against a diffuse grid of
wind-rippled foliage. Depthless, eerie. She adjusted her lenses to
look for heat sources. And saw nothing more than a few roosting
aviants and timid scavenger voles hardly larger than her thumb.

Nothing to lose sleep over. She turned her face to the sky again.

The brightest star wasn't a star at all. It was a planet, named
Cronos by some unimaginative Terrestrial number-bender when
it was detected a century ago: the Isian system's enormous gas giant,

currently at the aphelion of its looping orbit. Cronos had contributed to Isian geohistory by sweeping the system of its rocky and icy debris; comets were rare in the Isian sky. Less a Titan, Zoe thought, than a fat guardian angel.

Her inner-ear com link came alive, hissing faintly.

"Zoe?" Tam Hayes' voice. "Your telemetry puts you outside the tent and your pulse rate is up, so I assume you're awake."

"I don't walk in my sleep, if that's what you mean."

But she was immensely relieved to hear his voice.

"Restless?"

"A little. Is that a problem?"

"No problem."

The smallness of his voice inside her head made her even more aware of her position, alone in an alien forest. True, Yambuku wasn't far away; but Yambuku was a sealed environment, a fragile bubble of Earth. She had left that bubble and she was outside of it, lost on Isis. On Isis, where there were no artificial lights, no roads, no amenities over the next horizon. Nothing over the horizon but more horizon, parallax to parallel; nothing between her and a planetary Level Five hot zone but a membrane a few molecules thick. Unsurprising then that Devices and Personnel had chosen to resurrect her genome from the old diaspora stock. Isis was at least as lonely as any barren Kuiper object. And much, much farther from home.

"Zoe?"

"I'm here."

"We have a large animal paralleling your position, maybe fifty meters north-northwest. Nothing to worry about, but to avoid advertising your presence we'd like you to sit still for a few minutes."

"Back to the tent?"

"We'll keep you outside and mobile for now. Though I do wish you'd checked in before taking a walk. Just stay put, please, and let the tractibles do their work."

"Is this thing *stalking* me?"

"Probably just curious. Quiet, please."

She listened into the darkness but heard nothing. What kind of large animal? Most likely a triraptor, she supposed. She pictured it:

eight-limbed, quadripedal, with four arms on its erect upper body and claws like tempered steel. Her excursion suit was tough enough to protect her from the bites of small animals and invertebrates but not from the industrial-strength carnage of a triraptor attack.

"Zoe?"

She whispered, "I thought you wanted me quiet."

"We're okay as long as we don't shout. Can you make yourself comfortable out there?"

She scanned the ground, located a fallen tree trunk and sat down on it. Tiny insects from a disturbed nest swarmed over her footgear. Harmless things. She ignored them. " 'Comfortable' is relative. At least we can talk. Taking the night shift again?"

"Midnight to dawn, as long as you're on excursion."

She was flattered, not to mention intimidated. She had been thinking—could not help thinking—of her encounter with Hayes in the prep room, how she had wept in his arms at the news of the oceanic tragedy, and how she had found her way to his cabin that night. Of the way he had touched her, eagerly but gently, a way she had never been touched by another human being.

And she had permitted it.

Encouraged it.

Dreaded it.

"Little scary out there? Your pulse rate's up again."

She blushed—invisibly, thank God, unless the telemetry revealed that too. "It's just . . . dark a long way in every direction."

"Understood."

A wind from the west turned leaves in the trees. The same wind no doubt carried her scent deeper into the forest. No, don't think about that. "Tam?"

"Yes?"

"You grew up in the Kuipers. Red Thorn, you said?"

"Right. Red Thorn's a big KB habitat in the Near Oorts, one of the oldest Kuiper settlements. Three-quarters G spin around the long axis, so I didn't have to adapt much for Isis."

"Happy childhood?"

There was a pause. "Happy enough."

"Crèche or biofamily?"

"Bio. No crèches in Red Thorn; we're conservative."

"You miss the habitat?"

"Often."

He was being careful, she realized. Thinking of her, of her difficult childhood. "You know, it wasn't as bad for me as you might think. Being a crèche baby. Before Tehran, anyway. I liked being with my sisters, my nannies."

"Miss it?"

"Some things you can't get back. That feeling of . . . being where you belong."

"Nobody belongs on Isis."

The skin of her excursion suit was exquisitely sensitive, too much so. She startled at the touch of a falling leaf on her shoulder.

"Zoe?"

"Sorry. False alarm. There's a breeze up. Feels like it might rain soon." She wondered why it should be easier to talk to Hayes through the com link than face-to-face. "I know what I must seem like to a Kuiper person. Raised the way I was, I mean."

"None of us chose his childhood, Zoe."

"Like one of those old-time Chinese aristocratic women, her feet crammed into tiny shoes—do you know what I mean? Bent into someone else's idea of beauty or utility."

"Zoe . . ." He paused. "Old Kuiper maxim: 'A broken human being isn't even a good tool.' You couldn't have survived the way you did without something solid at the center of you, something all your own."

Now it was her turn to pause.

Theo used to say, *You're playing hide-and-seek, Zoe. Hiding from me again.*

But Theo always ferreted out her secrets.

Most of them.

Hayes said, "Quiet now, Zoe, just a while longer. The target turned your way again. The tractibles will lure it away, but don't call attention to yourself. And switch off your night vision, please, Zoe. The lenses leak; your eyes are glowing like a cat's."

"You can see me?" She wasn't sure she liked the idea.

"I'm monitoring one of the remensors. Hush now. I'll keep you updated."

She sighed and switched off the photon multiplier. Instantly, the dark became absolute. She closed her eyes and listened.

The wind was stronger now. Clouds had obscured the stars. A cold front was pushing in from the west, according to this morning's meteorological report. Raindrops began to spatter the forest canopy.

There was a rustling sound in the undergrowth, maybe a few meters away. Her pulse ramped up yet again.

Hayes said, "That's a tractible, guarding your flank. I know you can't see anything. But I need you to keep calm right now, to keep as still as you can."

She couldn't see the triraptor nosing through the forest but her excursion suit reported its scent—not the actual airborne molecules, of course, but an electronic tickling of the appropriate receptor cells, a faint echo of something acrid and bitter in her nose.

The animal was close. Night-hardened remensors buzzed around her. She heard, at last, the unmistakable sound of something alive and massive moving through the brush.

"Steady, Zoe."

Theo had taught her better discipline than this. She opened her eyes wide and imagined she saw it, the triraptor—the eyes of it, at least, glinting in a last wash of starlight from the eastern sky, classic predator's eyes, chrome-yellow and alert.

And gone.

"Keep still, Zoe."

Chasing some spider tractible, no doubt.

"A while longer."

The sounds retreated.

Cautiously, she turned her face up to the misting rain.

"I miss Elam," she whispered.

"I know, Zoe. I do too."

"We're running out of time, aren't we?"

"Let's hope not."

ELEVEN

DEGRANDPRE HAD PLANNED to give Avrion Theophilus the full tour of the IOS—when had there been such a guest as Avrion Theophilus? but the Devices and Personnel man was having none of it.

"What I want to see this morning," Theophilus had said mildly, "is your shuttle quarantine."

And what a grand scion of the Families this Theophilus had turned out to be! Tall, bone-thin, gray-haired, aquiline of nose and fashionably pale of complexion. Degrandpre's orchidectomy badge, which so impressed his subordinates, was nothing to this man but a servant's tattoo. No doubt Theophilus had already sired a brood of young aristocrats, strapping creatures with blue eyes and immaculate teeth.

Admirable, powerful! And potentially very dangerous. Avrion Theophilus was a Devices and Personnel functionary of unknown rank who conducted himself with all the arrogance of a Works Trust official, and that in itself was deeply confusing.

The news from Earth was equally troubling. Hints of turmoil among the Houses and the Families, show trials, perhaps a purge in the Trusts. But news through the particle-pair link was heavily censored, and although this Theophilus must know far more about the crisis than anyone onboard the IOS did, he hadn't volunteered to talk about it.

And Degrandpre dared not ask, for fear of seeming impertinent.

It was all so maddeningly ambiguous. Should he court the favor of Avrion Theophilus, or would that appear as a betrayal to his sponsors in the Works Trust? Was there a middle path?

An oppressive emotional atmosphere gripped the IOS, much as Degrandpre tried to minimize it. The loss of the Oceanic Station weighted heavily on staff even here; by all accounts, the surface personnel had grown brutally dispirited. Some saw it as the end of the human presence on Isis. And that it might well be, although this Theophilus seemed disturbingly indifferent. "Your orbital station needs some maintenance," Theophilus remarked blandly. "The ring corridor is filthy, and the air isn't much better."

The walls were dirty, true. Cleaning servitors had lately been scavenged for the interferometer project; replacements had not yet arrived from the Turing factories. As for the smell—"We've had some trouble with the scrubbers in our waste-management stacks. Temporary, of course, but in the meantime . . . I apologize. One grows accustomed to it."

"Perhaps not as easily as one might hope."

Perfect aristocratic tone, Degrandpre thought: insult and menace in a single phrase. He promised to see to the problem, though he couldn't imagine what he could do except bother the engineers yet again. No spares had arrived with the Higgs sphere, and he cynically wondered if replacements had been set aside to make room for the noble mass of Avrion Theophilus.

He escorted his guest as far as the massive bulkhead doors dividing Shuttle Quarantine from the rest of the IOS. Theophilus proceeded to inspect the seals and the rivet heads in minute detail, making Degrandpre wait. "As I'm sure you're aware," Degrandpre hinted, "these are the standard bulkheads; the sterile perimeter is inside."

"Nevertheless, I want these bulkheads inspected daily. By qualified engineers." At Degrandpre's shocked expression he added, "I don't think the Works Trust will disapprove, do you?"

Degrandpre palmed the admit button and the bulkhead door wheeled open. Inside, a single Kuiper-born medical engineer monitored the quarantine from a steel chair. The four survivors of the deep-sea disaster, a shuttle pilot and three junior marine exobiologists, had been languishing in containment for ten days now. A monitor image from the isolation chamber filled the screen above Degrandpre's head: two men, two women, all haggard in lab whites except for the pilot, whose Trust uniform was still relatively crisp.

Theophilus asked the medical engineer pointed and knowledgeable questions about quarantine procedures, redundancy, failsafes, alarm systems. Degrandpre took note but could infer nothing from the exchange . . . except that perhaps Devices and Personnel had grown nervous about the sterile status of the IOS.

But there had never been any question of that. Yes, it would be disastrous if there were an outbreak aboard the orbital station. The steel necklace of the IOS contained and nurtured nearly fifteen hundred human souls, and there was no plausible escape route for most of them; the planet below was universally toxic and the single spare Higgs launcher reserved for emergencies would carry a mere handful of managers at best. But there had never been even the hint of such a threat. Shuttles from Isis passed through the sterilizing vacuum of space, and cargo and passengers were rigorously quarantined and scrutinized. As the medical engineer patiently explained. And further explained. And continued to explain, until Degrandpre was forced to express his hope that the senior manager from Earth wasn't overwhelmed by all this perhaps unnecessary detail.

"Not at all," Theophilus said crisply. "Standard quarantine is ten days?"

The medical engineer nodded.

"And when will this one be finished?"

"Just a few hours from now, and no sign of contagion, nothing at all. They've been through a lot, these four; they're looking forward to release."

"Give them another week," Avrion Theophilus said.

"Master Theophilus," Degrandpre asked, "is there anything else you would like to see? The gardens perhaps, or the medical facilities?"

"Isis," Theophilus said.

They always want a window. "I can recommend the view from the docking bays."

"Thank you, but I'll be needing a closer look than that."

Degrandpre frowned. "Closer? You mean . . . you want to visit a ground station?"

Theophilus nodded.

My God, Degrandpre thought. He'll kill himself. On top of everything else, this grand, stupid Family cousin will kill himself, and the Families will blame *me*.

TWELVE

ZOE SLEPT LATE on the last morning of her three-day trial excursion. Her sleep had been irregular ever since the death of Elam Mather, shallow and florid with dreams, but exhaustion had tipped her into a black, dreamless unconsciousness. By the time she woke, her A.M. check-in from Yambuku was more than an hour late.

Are they letting me sleep, Zoe wondered, or had there been some new crisis, perimeter breach, disaster . . . ? She toggled her corneal display and called up a status report. The customary Yambuku telechatter scrolled past, tractibles talking to tractibles, but her personal com line showed a yellow hold tag. She queried the system and got a prerecorded note from Tam Hayes. He was involved, he said, in a conference with the IOS's kachos; he would talk to her shortly; in the meantime she might as well finish packing her campsite for the day's hike.

She stepped out of the tent into morning sunlight, feeling vaguely abandoned.

Her trial excursion had been an unqualified success. All the peripherals—tent, tractibles, food and waste-management systems, com links—had functioned so flawlessly that the Yambuku engineers were frankly envious. There was still hope for the human presence on Isis, even if the first-generation outposts had begun to fail. She was fulfilling her mission goals, and better than that, she was *in Isis*, mobile in the bios, just a stone's throw from the rushing Copper River. . . .

And why did that seem such hollow consolation?

Something's wrong with me, Zoe thought.

She deflated the tent walls, rolled the gel floors carefully and stored them on the back of a dog-sized cargo tractible. She packed her camp litter—empty food containers, a discharged power supply—although she could have buried it. The litter was sterile, but it would have been an intrusion, an insult to Isis.

Something's wrong. Oh, nothing physical; her perimeters were intact; she was as invulnerable to the bios as a human being could be. But something less tangible than a virus or a prion had begun to turn and move inside her.

The forest glistened with last night's rainfall. Water cycled from tier to tier of the tree canopy, overflowing from cupped leaves and flower chalices. In the shadowed spaces around the tree boles, the moisture had drawn out dozens of fungal fruiting bodies. Mold spores swirled in the westerly breeze, a fine sticky dust, like charcoal.

Should she speak to a doctor? If all went as planned, she would be back at Yambuku by nightfall. But her complaints were essentially minor—restlessness, disturbed sleep, and a host of uneasy feelings, not the least of which was her sexual liaison with Tam Hayes. Mention that to a physician at Yambuku and she would be in for a battery of endocrine and neurotransmitter tests, and did she want that? "No," she said aloud, the sound of her voice veiled by the suit filters but loud in the whispery glade. No, she *didn't* want that, and not just because of the physical inconvenience. To be honest, she was changing in ways that were as tantalizing as they were disturbing.

Her feelings about Hayes, for instance. She understood human sexuality well enough; she had studied it extensively. Her bioregulators kept her on an even keel chemically, but she was hardly sexless; the tantra instructors at the Middle School had praised her skills. No: what was shocking was that she had actually allowed him to *touch* her, had *wanted* him to touch her, had relished his touch. The Devices and Personnel clinicians had told her she would never have a satisfying orgasm with another human being. Her years in Tehran had built up too many negative associational paths, and anyway, her bioregulation damped the necessary hormonal feedback loops. She simply could not experience pleasurable intercourse with an adult male.

Or so they said.

So something was wrong. So she ought to alert a physician.

But she didn't want to. A physician might *fix* her, and the odd thing—the really disturbingly odd thing—was that she didn't *want* to be fixed.

If they fixed her she might not feel this shiver of anticipation at the sound of Tam's voice, the sudden weightlessness when he offered a compliment, the shocking intimacy of his hand on her body.

Madness, of course, but it had something of the divine in it. She wondered if she had stumbled across some wisdom lost to the modern world, an archaic emotional vector hidden under the stern sexual gridmaps of the Families or the chimp-like copulations of the Kuiper Clans.

Maybe this was how the unregulated proles fell in love. Did "love" feel like this, she wondered, in the viral hotlands of Africa and Asia?

She dreaded the feeling. And she dreaded the idea that it might one day stop.

By noon, the camp was packed and ready. Still no word from Yambuku. She needed to leave within the hour or risk reaching the station after dark.

She left a call-me memo for Hayes with Dieter Franklin, who was monitoring her stats and vitals. Luckily the forest was calm this morning, no predators within her scannable radius, white clouds riding the meridian like slow boats on a tide.

She assembled her party of six-legged tractibles and set off westward. The path, beaten by machines in advance of her excursion, followed the shore of the Copper for a half-klick or so. This time of year, the river ran shallow. The water had pulled back from its banks to reveal stony fords, quiescent green pools, and silt dunes where a few venturous weeds had taken root. Automated insect remensors followed her in a cloud like circling gnats; some flew ahead, monitoring the route. The faint buzz of them was lost in the cacophony of bird and insect calls, all of which sounded alike to her, power lines buzzing in a heat wave.

Her excursion suit tunneled beads of sweat from her skin to the membrane's surface, cooling her as she walked. Sunlight turned the membrane white. She glanced at her arms. She was as pale as a purebred daughter of some Nordic Family, aristocratic white.

She had not traveled more than a kilometer when Tam Hayes opened a direct link to her. About time, she thought.

"Zoe? We'd like you to halt where you are for the time being."

"Can't," she said. "Not if I want to be back before dark. You've been talking to the IOS all morning. Time doesn't stop just because Kenyon Degrandpre is keeping you busy."

"That's the point. They want the excursion extended."

They, she noted. Not *we*. Hayes didn't approve. "What do you mean, extended?"

"Specifically, they want you to turn back, cross the Copper at the mobile bridge and break camp on the east bank. Remensors will scout a path to the digger colony, and the tractibles will trailblaze for you. Two days of traveling ought to put you just inside the animals' food-gathering perimeter."

Which was absurd. "I can't do fieldwork! We're still testing the excursion gear!"

"Feeling at the IOS is that your gear passed all the tests."

"This pushes the schedule by at least a month."

"Somebody's in a hurry, I guess."

She supposed she knew why. The Oceanic Station had collapsed and all the other Isian outposts had suffered worrisome seal failures. Zoe's excursion suit might be performing brilliantly, but without a staging platform like Yambuku, it was as useful as a rain-hat in a hurricane. The Trusts wanted to maximize the use of her before Yambuku had to be evacuated.

Cross the Copper River toward the foothills? Move deeper into the bios while Yambuku staggered toward collapse? Was she brave enough to do that?

"Personally," Hayes said, "I'm opposed to the idea. I don't have the authority to overrule it, but we can always find an anomaly in your gear and order you back for maintenance."

"But the suit is flawless. You said so yourself."

"Oh, I think Kwame Sen could be convinced to shade a graph or two if it came to an argument."

She thought about it. "Tam, who gave this order? Was it De-grandpre?"

"He sanctioned it, but no, the order came from your D-and-P man—Avrion Theophilus."

Theo!

Surely *Theo* wouldn't let anything bad happen to her.

She capped her doubts. "Keep Kwame honest. I'll cross the river."

"Zoe? Are you sure about this?"

"Yes."

No.

"Well . . . I'm sending out three more tractibles with supplies and equipment. They should catch up with you by dusk. And as far as I'm concerned, you're on immediate recall at the first sign of trouble. Any kind of trouble. Give me the word, I'll cover it with the IOS."

He added, "I'll be watching," which made her feel both strong and weak at once, and signed off.

Zoe gazed across the placid Copper. Her pack tractibles acknowledged a new set of orders from Yambuku by circling back behind her, ambling up the trail like dimly impatient dogs and waiting for her to follow.

. . .

The bridge over the Copper River was a string of logs spun to-gether with strands of high-tensile monofilament and anchored at either end with spikes driven deep into the gravelly soil. It was sturdy enough, Zoe supposed, but makeshift, not meant to last. Mild as the seasons on Isis were, another few weeks would see monsoon rains swelling the Copper to its limits, and this small spec-imen of tractible engineering would be washed away and dispersed.

The bridge crossed the Copper at a broad and shallow place where, if she looked between the slats, she could see the polished river rocks and the quiet places where creatures not quite fish— they looked like overgrown tadpoles—swarmed and spawned. She could have forded the river here, she was certain, without any bridge at all. Some of her cargo tractibles did just that, managing the water with their javelin legs more surely than they could have navigated these loosely strung logs.

Across the river the trail was less obvious; it had not been as completely blazed as the path to the bridge. By their nature the tractibles passed delicately over the landscape; it took a great deal of mechanical effort to flatten a patch of grass, much less to clear away tangled undergrowth. She would have to proceed more care-fully here. The excursion suit's membrane was strong enough to resist tearing under any ordinary circumstance, but a sharp enough pressure—a knife blade with some strength behind it, a large pred-ator's claws, or a fall from a height—might open a seam.

She doubted she would have trouble with knives. As for pred-ators, the tractibles and insect remensors would watch out for her. And in any case these rocky foothills were not as inviting a hunting ground as the savanna that stretched to the south and west. Trirap-tors were dangerous but uncommon here; the smaller, faster car-nivores were about the size of house cats and easily frightened away from something as large and unfamiliar as a human being. That was perhaps one reason the digger colony had thrived here.

And as for heights—well, she would be reluctant to press far beyond the diggers' rangeland, into the hills where the Copper

River ran in narrow, fast channels among slate-sharp rocks. Short of that, she was confident of her footing.

What was left to fear?

Any of ten thousand unsuspected events, Zoe thought. Not to mention her own state of mind.

Not that she felt bad. The opposite. Her moods had been mercurial, but right now she felt surprisingly good, felt solid, walking in the sunlight and swinging her arms with a freedom she hadn't felt since crèche. The trail followed a low ridge eastward; when the ridge rose high enough she was able to see the canopy of the forest sloping to the west, as dense and close as a well-kept secret. All of this touched her—she didn't have a better word—in a way she had thought impossible, as if when she left Yambuku, she had not donned a protective membrane but stripped one away. She was as raw as a nerve; the simple blue sky made her want to weep with joy.

She could think of no explanation for these mood shifts . . . unless she was deregulating. Could that be? But thymostats were simple homeostatic machines; she had never heard of a bioregulator malfunction. Anyway, wouldn't it have shown up on her medical telemetry?

Doesn't matter, some traitorous part of her whispered. She was alive—truly alive for the first time in many years—and she *liked* it.

Liked it almost as much as she feared it.

She halted well before dusk at one of the potential campsites mapped into the tractibles' memory. The ridgetop broadened here into a stony plateau, tufts of green succulents poking through the topsoil between slabs of glacial rock. Pitching the tent was easy— the tent was smart enough to do most of the work itself—but anchoring it proved more difficult. She drove stakes into stony cracks and soil-filled hollows, tethering her shelter the old-fashioned way. She queried Yambuku for a weather report, but nothing had changed since this morning: skies clear, winds calm. Isis was showing her gentle aspect.

She checked in with Dieter after a hasty meal. No real news, Dieter said, except that this Avrion Theophilus, the Devices and Personnel mystery man, was due down on the next shuttle.

Theo at Yambuku, Zoe thought.

Given her mood, she guessed that should have made her happy. She wondered why it didn't.

The sun drifted behind the Copper Mountains. Zoe finished the ungainly process of eating through the excursion suit and was ready to make another assault on the citadel of sleep when an alert popped into her corneal display. The voice of Yambuku this time was Lee Reisman, who had taken over the shift from Dieter. "We have a large animal on your perimeter," Lee said, then: "Oh! It's a digger!"

She was instantly alert. "Is it approaching the tent?"

"No . . . according to the remensors, it's holding about a hundred yards off your location. Tractibles are positioned to intercept it, but—"

"Leave it alone for now," Zoe said.

"Zoe? This isn't an appropriate time to initiate contact."

"I just want a look."

She climbed out of the tent, her vision augmented in the deepening dusk. Slate rocks radiated the day's heat like embers. She had thought the digger might be hard to see, but she spotted it at once and increased the amplification in her membrane lenses accordingly.

It—make that *he*—was already a familiar presence: this was the digger Hayes had called "Old Man." She recognized the white whiskers, the splay of tendrils under its eyes.

She looked at Old Man, and Old Man looked back at her.

It was, of course, impossible to read any emotion into that face, as much as the human mind wanted to try. We project ourselves onto other animals, Zoe thought; we see expression in the faces of cats and dogs; but the digger was as inscrutable as a lobster. The eyes, she thought. On any creature larger than a beetle, the eyes are the primary vehicle of expression; but the digger's eyes were simple black ovals in a bed of bony flesh. Bubbles of ink. Windows through which some dim not-quite-sentience regarded her coolly.

"Old Man," she whispered. The curious one.

Old Man blinked—a flash of silver over shimmering black— then turned and loped away.

THIRTEEN

W HAT HAYES HAD not told Zoe was that cascading seal failures had kept him busy most of the day. He could not help wishing that Mac Feya were still here to lend a hand—Mac had been good at patching seals. Barring the one that had killed him.

Lee, Sharon, and Kwame were more than competent engineers, but they were overtaxed and running on minimum sleep. For now, the situation had been stabilized—replacement seals installed and samples from the failed gaskets glove-boxed for analysis. Hayes had been following the work closely. Dieter Franklin took Hayes into his laboratory to look at adaptive changes in the bacteria feeding on the gaskets, the increasing density of fibrillary matter in the body of the cell, microtubules coiled like DNA where, a month ago, there had been only a few stray threads. The granular bodies on the cell surface were also novel, synthesizing and excreting highly polar molecules, digging into their environment. Dieter waved a hand at the screen he had called up: "It's not the same organism we were looking at six months ago."

"Same genome," Hayes said. "Same organism."

"Same genome, but it's expressing itself in a radically different way."

"So it's environmentally sensitive."

"At the very least. Might as well say it's trying to pry open the station and come inside."

Dieter was Gamma Stone Clan, given to overstatement. "If they're growing, it's because we're feeding them."

"They're dying as fast as they grow."

True enough. Hayes had spent his share of time in excursion gear, scrubbing decayed bacterial mats from the station's exposed surfaces. Kamikaze bacteria? "I don't think they literally want to kill us, Dieter."

"That might be a dangerous assumption to make."

Hayes was famous for the hours he kept. People said he never slept.

Lately that had been all too true. He had personally supervised much of Zoe's ongoing excursion, not to mention coordinating the seal repairs and a complete changeover on one of the big filter stacks. He was averaging four or five hours of sleep per night and was often grateful to get that much. Sleep deprivation had left him testy and hypersensitive. For the first time in his life, he envied the Terrestrial hands who wore thymostats. He had to make do with caffeinated drinks and willpower, the poor man's equivalent.

It was late when he left Dieter Franklin's laboratory. Almost everyone but the graveyard shift had retired for the night. At night, the station seemed both too large and too small—the echo of his footsteps came back to him as if from a vast space, but the sound was flat, contained: a *closed* space. Every avenue a dead end.

Yambuku had never seemed so fragile.

His research notes lay untouched in his cabin. He was tempted to go there now, but a last task awaited him, one he had been putting off. This Terrestrial D&P kacho was due down in the morning and would need fresh quarters. But there was only one vacancy at Yambuku, and that was the cabin Elam Mather had occupied.

Cleaning it out for Avrion Theophilus was a simple enough chore. No one on Isis owned anything substantial. The joke was, you came to Isis the way you came into the world: naked and afraid. And left the same way.

Elam had left rather differently, but she had taken nothing with her. Still, the sheets needed to be laundered and the wall screens cleared of personal displays.

Small work, but not work he relished. Nor could it be delegated. When a hand died, the station manager always cleared the cabin. He had done the same thing for Mac Feya. Any old hand would; it was one of the few customs the Isis Project had developed.

He let himself into the cabin with his master key.

Elam's desk light winked on as he stepped inside, then so did the wall screen—a live image of Isis relayed from orbit. Was this how Elam had liked to imagine herself, out of the toxic bios, above it all? Or had she simply preferred to take the long view?

He switched off the screen and dumped Elam's preferences back into the station pool. Then he collected and folded her sheets and took the issue garments from her shelves. All were of the uniform ultralight charcoal-colored cloth imported from Earth. He put them outside the door for a tractible robot to pick up. Elam's laundry would cycle interchangeably through the Yambuku housekeeping system; in a day or two, he might be sleeping on one of these same sheets.

Last, he used his scroll to open Elam's personal memory cache in Yambuku's core memory. Mac had left his filestack full of random notes to himself, letters home, indecipherable notes. Elam was tidier than that; likely all that remained to be cleared would be lists, schedules, and access numbers.

But when he asked for a global delete, one item came up red-tagged.

It was a message, unfinished, and it was addressed to him.

Tam,

Currently skimming over the ocean on the way to meet Freeman Li. Realized we hadn't had an opportunity to talk lately. Can we get together as soon as I'm back? Until then, some thoughts.

No doubt you remember when I told you to steer clear of Zoe Fisher. Maybe I was wrong. (Shows how much my motherly advice is worth, I guess.) There is something special about that girl, I agree, but you have to understand, Tam— her specialness makes her dangerous. Maybe very dangerous.

And yes, I know she's innocent of any personal scheming. Just as obviously, though, she's a tool in some complicated Devices and Personnel power play. This is bad news for her, God knows, and might be trouble for you too, given the interest you've taken in her. Please don't be naive! The Trust uses people like Zoe Fisher the way you and I use toilet paper. The only thing that protects us here is distance, and even that might not protect us much longer. Isis isn't a republic; it's a Trust property. Never forget that.

This Avrion Theophilus is suddenly on a cargo manifest from Earth. Part of a plan—or worse, a plan gone wrong. Watch out for him, Tam. Trust Families don't send a fancy cousin like that on such a dangerous journey unless the stakes are very, very high. Maybe he only wants to make sure Zoe succeeds—that the excursion gear functions as promised—but even if that's so, it means there must be equally powerful people who want her to fail.

But here is the truly troublesome news: I think Zoe's bloodware has been tampered with.

Last night I found her in the cargo hold, about an hour after midnight. She thought she was alone, and she was crying. Quiet, helpless baby tears—you know the kind I mean. When

I asked her what was wrong, she blushed and mumbled something about a nightmare. What struck me was the way she said it, trying to sound casual, obviously attempting to brush me off, but weirdly sincere, too, as if a nightmare was a completely novel experience, something she had only read about in books. Which it might well be, given her D&P background.

Ask yourself, Tam: Why should a highly regulated bottle baby like Zoe Fisher suddenly suffer from nightmares? (Or fall in love, come to that!)

After I calmed down Zoe and chased her back to bed, I woke up Shel Kyne. Shel is a competent physician but he's irredeemably Terrestrial. He didn't even wonder why I was asking all these questions about Zoe's bloodware—just trotted out her charts, miffed at the hour but happy to be consulted. (I don't know about you Red Thorns, but among Rider Clan the unwarranted sharing of medical information is grounds for summary disenfranchisement. Earthlings!)

I asked, first, whether emotional instability might be a sign of a failing thymostat.

Yes, Shel tells me, that's certainly possible, though thymostatic disequilibrium can be subtle at the beginning; emotional volubility doesn't usually show up until some weeks or even months after the thymostat switches off.

So I asked him. Is there anything wrong with Zoe's regulator?

He smiled and said he didn't know.

Apparently Zoe is loaded with novel bloodware, most of it in genned gland sacs clustered around the abdominal aorta. These devices are so newfangled that Shel's instruments won't read them, and D&P didn't send blueprints. The most Shel can do is monitor her metabolites for the major neurotransmitters and regulatory chemistry. Zoe's serotonin, dopamine, norepinephrine, and Substance P do look a little odd, apparently, and she's negative for most of the common reuptake inhibitors. But her regulatory bloodware is so unusual that Shel can't decide if this is appropriate functioning or a major malfunction.

Shel suggested we ask Avrion Theophilus about it when he arrives. (I lied and said I would; I also advised Shel to keep quiet about it until I spoke to him again. You might want to edit his reports to the IOS in the next little while.)

So what does this mean?

It means, I suspect, that Zoe is off her thymostat, maybe for the first time in her life. In Kuiper terms, she's practically a newborn. A whole battery of new and difficult emotions to cope with, and she doesn't understand any of it. The Zoe Fisher you're so obviously falling in love with, Tam, is a brand-new Zoe Fisher. Fragile. Probably scared. And trying very hard to do the job she's been trained for.

I can't tell you what to do about any of this. I don't know.

My only useful advice: Keep your eyes open.

Watch your back.

I'll do the same. I'm saving this into my personal memory, because I don't want it drifting through Yambuku cyberspace. If all goes well, we can talk in person as soon as I'm back.

—Elam

P.S. Of course she likes you, you idiot! Many of us do. Myself included. Were you too dense to notice, or too polite to let on?

Idle curiosity.

Hayes read the message.

Then he read it again, enclosed in the silence of what had once been Elam's cabin, as night rolled over the long valleys and the canopied hills.

FOURTEEN

W HEN THE RED-LIGHT summons from the shuttle's
quarantine module appeared on his scroll, Corbus Nefford was mildly scandalized. There had never been a
medical crisis aboard the IOS during his health-management watch,
and he fully intended that there never would be.

Admittedly, this didn't look good—an unexplained summons
of the highest priority posted by Ken Kinsolving, day-watch quarantine medic, from the shuttle-bay lockdown. Dire as that sounded,
however, it was probably only Kinsolving panicked by some crewman's gastritis attack or tension headache. The alternative was un-
thinkable.

But he found a guard stationed at the shuttle module's bulkhead
door, and inside—

Inside, there was chaos.

Two nursing assistants sat plugged into remensor hoods, talking
through their microphones in low, urgent tones. Kinsolving, gaunt
in his drapery of medical whites, waved Nefford toward an empty

control bay. "Rios and Soto are dead," he said flatly. "Raman is comatose and Mavrovik is intermittently lucid. We need help with palliative care and tissue samples—if you would, Manager."

Kinsolving was a junior medic and not entitled to speak to Corbus Nefford quite so brusquely, but this was an emergency, after all. Nefford squirmed into the remensor chair. He had put on some weight since the last time he operated one of these rigs.

But one did what one must. What one was trained for, and thank God for his training; it supplanted the instinct to panic. He imagined his thymostat registering the sudden torrents of epinephrine, working to calm him without dulling his heightened alertness. Pathogens, he found himself thinking, Isian pathogens aboard the IOS: it was the nightmare he had hoped never to face. . . .

The remensor hood activated and he was suddenly inside the quarantine room with the victims. His arms had become the arms of a medical tractible and his eyes were its enhanced sensors. He oriented himself quickly. The quarantine chamber was claustrophobically small, never meant to be used as a hospital ward. Tractibles and remensors battled for floor space; Kinsolving's remensor rolled up next to him.

He identified the shuttle crewmen on their cots. Mavrovik, Soto, Raman, and Rios. Two male, two female. They had been the sole survivors of the oceanic disaster, a pilot and three crewmen who had shuttled up from the outpost shortly before its final collapse.

And they had brought something with them, apparently, although they had been in quarantine with no observable ill effects for, what was it, most of a month now? And didn't Isian pathogens attack almost instantly? An Isian infectious agent with a long incubation period was unheard of—a threat almost too terrifying to contemplate.

He followed Kinsolving's medical remensor to the bedside of the shuttle pilot, Mavrovik. Kinsolving had plugged fluids and hemostats into Mavrovik's exposed arm. Nefford added a pulmonary tap to drain blood and fluid from the pilot's lungs. Mavrovik had been disrobed and strapped to the cot. Beads of sweat, putrid and faintly yellow, trickled down his shaved skull to his pillow.

What Kinsolving had achieved here was a momentary homeostasis. Nefford plugged his own monitors into the shuttle pilot as the day-shift medic began to transfer control. When a moment of peace presented itself he asked, "How long have they been ill?"

"First obvious symptoms manifested about three hours ago. We had no real warning. Their blood gasses looked peculiar prior to that, but still within normal limits."

Nefford turned to watch as two tractibles shifted the stiffening bodies of Rios, a woman, and Soto, a man, onto gurneys and wheeled them out of the room. There was a cold-storage facility with an autopsy chamber deep inside the quarantine boundary— staffed, of course, entirely by tractibles and remensors. The morgue was carefully maintained, although it hadn't been used before today.

When he turned back he found Mavrovik's eyes open, both pupils grossly dilated. Sweating inside his remensor hood, Nefford scrolled a survey of the patient's vital signs. The list was appalling. Gross edema, internal bleeding as tissues softened catastrophically, kidneys necrotizing, liver function fading, pulse erratic, blood pressure so uncertain that even the hemostatic robots could barely maintain an acceptable count. Bottom line: Mavrovik was dying. In a hurry.

Kinsolving wheeled back, his tractible arms going limp as he disengaged from the remensor hood. "Do what you can for him," he said flatly. "I'll speak to Degrandpre."

Better you than me, Nefford thought.

He assumed full life-support function as Kinsolving's medical remensor fell silent.

Mavrovik was briefly stabilized, but that wouldn't last. The trouble was, Nefford had no effective treatment for this disease— whatever it was—only palliatives, only bags of fresh artificial blood and coagulent nanobacters to seal the worst of the internal lesions. All useless in the long run. Mavrovik was being devoured by an entity Nefford could not even name, and soon enough it would do irreparable damage to Mavrovik's heart or brain, and that would be that.

As if he had overheard the thought, Mavrovik gasped suddenly and surged against his restraints. Nefford flinched. Fortunately, his remensor ignored hasty autonomic impulses or he might have ripped an intravenous line out of the patient. *How I must look to him*, Nefford thought: a robotic head, a cow's skull dipped in chromium, peering at him through ruby lenses. But Mavrovik's eyes had closed; his lips moved, but he was talking to someone not present.

"Who are you?" the pilot demanded weakly, his throat thick with bloody granulae.

"Be still," Nefford said. Corbus Nefford's voice was relayed with ultimate fidelity through the remensor, that much of his bedside manner, at least, intact. He added a tranquilizer to the broth of chemicals in the shuttle pilot's drip.

But Mavrovik would not be tranquil. "Look at them!" His lips were flecked with blood. "Look at them!"

"Calm down, Mr. Mavrovik. Don't speak. Conserve your strength."

"So *many* of them!"

Nefford sighed and tightened the restraints. This might be, was probably, Mavrovik's final crisis. He pushed the flow of opiates.

"Talking, all talking together. . . ."

Corbus Nefford had not been in the presence of a dying man since his medical apprenticeship in Paris. Death was the business of hospices and peasant medics, not of successful Family physicians. He had forgotten how hair-raising the process could be. He peeled back Mavrovik's left eyelid, expecting to find the pupil fixed and dilated; instead, the pupil contracted promptly at the light. Then Mavrovik's right eye opened and the pilot looked at Nefford with a sudden, frightening lucidity.

"You have to understand this," Mavrovik said. He rasped the words through a lace of bloody sputum. *Like a dead man talking*, Nefford thought. Well, close enough. "There are thousands of

them. Hundreds of thousands. Talking to each other. Talking to
me!"

Nefford felt trapped by the sheer earnestness of this declama-
tion. He was aware of the patient's plummeting vascular pressure,
capillaries weakened by the disease bleeding out in a massive,
whole-body collapse. Mavrovik's face was banded with blue and
black, as if he had been beaten with a stick. The whites of his eyes
were shot through with scarlet. Mavrovik's brain must be bleeding
too, Nefford thought; this monologue could hardly be sane. But
he heard himself ask, "Thousands of *what*, Mr. Mavrovik?"

"Worlds," Mavrovik said, gently now, as if to himself.

Corbus Nefford did not, of course, believe in ghosts. He was
a technician of the Families—in his own way, a scientist. Only low
people and peasants were frightened of ghosts or spirits. Nefford
was frightened only of the Trusts. He had seen the damage they
could inflict.

Nevertheless he found himself regarding the dying man with
something approaching superstitious dread.

Mavrovik laughed—a terrible sound; it brought up bubbles of
pink fluid. Robotic aspirators sucked his mouth and throat clean.
His arms flexed against his restraints, as if he wanted to reach up,
to grasp Nefford—Nefford's remensor—and draw him closer.

Horrible thought.

"We're their orphans!" Mavrovik explained.

His last words.

Raman died too, more quietly, at about the same time. With the
deaths the quarantine room grew calmer, though frantic activity
continued—the drawing of blood and tissue samples, the containment of the bodies, periodic cloudbursts of liquid sterilants and
gases.

When Mavrovik's corpse was finally bagged and taken away,
Nefford allowed himself to draw a long breath. He wheeled his
remensor back into its dock and removed himself from the hood.

He had been with the remensor so long that his own body felt clumsy and unfamiliar. He had been sweating freely; his clothing was soaked; he recoiled at his own stink. He wanted a long drink of water and a hot bath. Probably he should have been hungry—he had missed breakfast—but the thought of food was repellent.

He found Kinsolving waiting for him near the bulkhead door. Nefford asked, "Did you talk to Degrandpre?"

"I paged his scroll . . ."

"Paged his scroll?" An event like this called for a personal conference. Nefford would have done it himself if he hadn't been busy with Mavrovik.

"Manager Degrandpre was already aware of the emergency. I asked to meet with him. But he had already issued an order expanding the perimeter of the quarantine." Kinsolving delivered this information meekly, as if he expected to be beaten for it.

"Expanding the perimeter? I don't understand."

"Quarantine extends all the way to the bulkhead doors. The entire module is sealed tight." Kinsolving bowed his head. "No one is allowed to leave until further notice. And that includes us."

T
HE DREAMS WERE very bad.
        Rain came down on the polyplex shelter in drumming
bursts. Wind gusts confused the support tractibles, which
woke Zoe periodically with false alarms, misinterpreting the whip-
ping wind as the movement of some ghostly predator. Zoe fell in
and out of shallow sleep.

She was, of course, still alone. She was as alone as the first
lungfish to drag itself out of the shallows. And that should have
been all right. The men and women who first sailed to the reefs of
the solar system, squandering their lives inside lightless ice caverns—
they had been alone too.

But isolation meant many things.

Zoe had known people who longed for isolation and people
who dreaded it. On Earth a person was never truly alone, and it
was easy to project a whole spectrum of fears and hopes into that
unobtainable void, a vacuum full of self. It meant freedom, or
shamelessness, or absolution, or the simple loss of all direction.

Fantasies.

Alone, Zoe thought, is listening to this rain batter the small membrane between herself and toxic nature. Alone meant memories swollen into nightmares.

In her dreams she was in Tehran.

According to the Trust doctors, these memories had been safely buried. But whatever was wrong with her seemed to have let slip the leash. Whenever she closed her eyes the awful images came roaring back.

The orphan crèche was a cinderblock dungeon spread across acres of oily gravel and ringed with lethal glass-wire fences. It was, like most of the charity crèches scattered across Asia and Europe, a leftover from the plague century. It might once have been a humanitarian project, one of the great Social Works of the first Trusts, but it had become little more than a collector for the state brothels. Lately its resident managers had realized that they could expand their personal profit margin by renting their charges on the public market, or at least that segment of the market too impoverished or ill to patronize the licensed pleasuredromes.

The drawback was that the inmates at the Tehran West Quad Educational Collective—as the sign above the gate proclaimed it— weren't offered the kind of medical supervision required even in a bargain-basement, licensed brothel. Nor were its customers, mainly manual laborers from the local Trust factories ringing the city, carefully screened.

Zoe had arrived with her pod of genetically identical sisters, Francesca and Poe and Avita and Lin, shipped from their birth crèche by orbital cargo transport, hungry and bewildered. At first the Farsi-speaking nurse had fed them protein soups and dressed them in warm if graceless smocks and patiently endured their demands for home. But after a day or two of this, they were transferred to the dormitories.

And the horror began.

Memory swept through Zoe's dreams like a winter gale.

Everyone was used, and everyone died.

Francesca died first, of a fever that wracked her body for five long February days, until she turned her emaciated body to the cinderblock wall and simply ceased to breathe.

This is wrong, Zoe remembered herself thinking. We were made to go to the stars. This is wrong.

Poe and Lin died together when a fierce hemorrhagic contagion—the nurses called it Brazzaville 3, which it may have been—swept the dormitories. Zoe, in her despair, had not felt much grief at the passing of three of her sisters. She was selfishly grateful that the brothel trade had diminished out of fear of the plague. Unfortunately the food supply had diminished too, and that wasn't good. There had been talk of quarantine; the whole West Quarter of the city was practically deserted for the next six months.

But the disease passed in time. Zoe and Avita were among the souls not harvested.

Zoe grew closer to her only remaining pod sister, and it affected her more powerfully when Avita died, almost randomly, of some disease born of malnutrition and neglect. She is my mirror, Zoe thought, gazing at Avita's corpse during the long hours before the hygiene crew came to collect it. When I die, Zoe thought—and she had supposed it would be a matter of months, at most—when I die, this is how I will look. Like a soft clay statue, pale and shiny and indifferent.

She missed Avita and Francesca and Lin and Poe. The other inmates were often cruel to her, and her white-masked minders casually despised her, and she thought death might not be so terrible, really, certainly no worse than living on and on inside these walls.

Then Theo came to Tehran.

Something had happened, something political, something in the High Families. She remembered Avrion Theophilus from the crèche. He had stopped by once a month to survey the pods, and he had been partial to the five small sisters, often stroking Zoe's hair while the nannies ducked their heads at him and dull-witted tractibles brought him tea and sugar cakes, which he shared. He had always looked so resplendent in his black uniform, and he looked resplendent now, in Tehran, but darker, angrier, shouting at the orphan keepers, who cringed away from him. He cursed the obscenties of the dormitory, the frigid showers, the assignation rooms with their coarse and filthy blankets.

He swept Zoe up into his arms—cautiously, because she had become fragile. His uniform, pressed against her cheek, smelled of fresh laundry, of soap and steam-pressing.

She thought of him as a kind of king or prince. Of course he was not—he was only peripherally of the Families at all, a cousin's nephew's cousin, essentially a high functionary with the Devices and Personnel branch of the Trusts. He was a Theophilus, not a Melloch or a Quantrill or a Mitsubishi. But that didn't matter. He had come to get her. Too late for Poe or Lin or Avita or Francesca. But not too late for Zoe.

"One of my girls survived," he murmured, carrying her out into a Human Services mobile clinic. "One of my girls survived."

When he tried to hand her to the doctors she clung to him so fiercely that she had to be sedated.

Zoe woke abruptly, numb with dread. There had been a sound . . . but it was only a rattle of thunder bouncing between the peaks of the high Coppers. Locally, the rain had slowed to a drizzle.

Dim light came through the polyplex shelter. Morning.

She felt shaky and tired. She opened the shelter and climbed out into the rain. Water sheeted off the granite outcrops and drenched the blades of the gorse-like plants that grew in the deep glacial scars. Pack-mule tractibles lurched comically about the campsite. Their legs found little purchase in the wet; periodically they folded their limbs and sat down like weary dogs.

Clouds tumbled up the Coppers in gusting billows. The forest steamed.

She selected a ration dispenser from the store aboard a nearby tractible and carried it back under cover. The rain had beaded on her excursion suit. She itched. The membrane kept her clean, even shuttled flakes of dead skin to its surface and shed them as sterile dust; nevertheless, she itched. The itch was intermittent, confined to her ribs and thighs, and was not a real problem—yet. But if it got worse . . . well, people had been known to claw themselves bloody in order to a cure an itch. Which, under the circumstances, wouldn't do. It wouldn't do at all.

Eating was a chore. The ration tube had to be attached to the excursion suit's face mask, which opened a sterile passage between mouth and food—agonizingly slowly. She compressed the ration tube by hand. The nutrient paste that oozed onto her tongue was fundamentally unappetizing and as perfectly textureless as mud. And never enough to convince her she had really eaten.

The rations also tended to pass through her body quickly, which presented her with another tedious and unpleasant problem.

By the time she finished with all this, the sky had begun to clear. The wind had grown gusty again, however; it dragged at the polyplex fabric and would no doubt be making life difficult for the robots and remensors.

She thought about calling Yambuku. Her check-in was due.

She thought about Theo, of how he had saved her from the orphan ranch, memories that had tumbled through her dreams like broken glass. . . .

And her inexplicable dread of him.

She linked to Yambuku for her daily update and spoke briefly to Cai Connor, who was manning the excursion desk. No news and stay put: the winds would diminish overnight and then she could reconnoiter the digger colony before heading back.

Which was fine, but it left her with nothing to do except monitor her own telltales, watch the cumulus clouds writhe up the distant peaks, and function-test the pack-mule tractibles.

She didn't look forward to another night of darkness.

That afternoon, Tam Hayes contacted her by narrow-beam transmission from Yambuku. *That* was odd. The tight-beam antenna was a last-ditch redundancy, limited to line of sight and narrow in bandwidth. Clunky, voice-only, like an antique telephone line.

"This is off the record," Hayes began. "Nobody's eavesdropping, and nothing we say goes into the station's memory. Zoe, are you in a safe place? I'm in the shuttle bay; I don't have a remensor view."

"Sitting in the shelter waiting for the wind to drop."

"Good. We have a lot to talk about."

"You start," Zoe said.

He began by reading her the contents of Elam Mather's message.

Zoe had entertained some of these suspicions herself. About the thymostat, anyway. "But it must have been functioning when I left Phoenix. The medical surveillance was extremely tight."

She thought of Anna Chopra, the Terrestrial physician who had presided over her health during the long pre-launch months. A tall woman, gray-haired, a non-Family functionary from Djakarta, was it? Grim and wordless and quite dedicated.

"Maybe an act of sabotage," Hayes suggested. "Some Family turf war working itself out."

Maybe, but Family feuds were seldom so subtle. An accident, more likely.

"The point is," Hayes went on, "you shouldn't be out there by yourself with a dead 'stat."

"If that's all you wanted to say, you could have said it wideband."

"Thought you might want to keep this private."

"Meaning you think I might want to stay this way. Unregulated. Like a Kuiper woman."

He left a silence in the distance between them. "Yes," he said at last, "maybe. It's your call, of course, Zoe."

My call, she thought. My choice.

But it begged too many questions. The thymostat regulated personality: Am I the same person I was three months ago?

So hard, Zoe thought, to hold yourself in your hand, weigh

yourself, render a judgment. She felt better. She felt worse. She said to Hayes, "You must have suspected something . . ."

"From time to time, but I'm Red Thorn; we don't wear thymostats and I've never been sure what to expect from people who do. Elam's been to Earth; she had better instincts."

"There are different kinds of thymostats. Mainly, they regulate mood, but mine did more than that, Tam. It suppressed unpleasant memories. It also displaced sexual impulses and directed that energy into my work."

"But you're functioning without it."

She reminded herself that no one could hear her. No one but Tam. "I feel like I'm on the edge all the time. Sleep is disturbed. I have mood swings. Sometimes this whole excursion seems futile and dangerous. Sometimes . . . I'm afraid."

Another long pause. Wind rattled the shelter.

"Zoe, we have medical spares. We can fix you up."

"No. I don't want that."

"You're certain?"

"I'm not certain of anything. But I don't want to go back to being . . . what I was."

What I was for Theo. What I was for the Trusts.

Hayes said, "I'll do everything in my power to keep this quiet. The risk is that Avrion Theophilus will look at your medical telemetry and figure it out for himself."

Better that than facing him, Zoe thought. *One look at me and he would know. He would see it in my eyes.*

"In any case, you're in no shape to spend another day in the field. I want you back here where I can look after you."

"No," Zoe said. "I'd rather finish this."

"It's not just the 'stat. I want you back here in case we're forced to evacuate."

"Evacuate Yambuku? Tam, is it that bad?"

"Things change quickly."

He described a series of cascading seal failures and filter-stack problems. *Everything crumbling,* Zoe thought. *Everything falling apart.* "Give me a day to think about it."

"It's another day's worth of risk."

"Nothing we do here is safe. Give me a day, Tam."

"You don't have to prove anything."

"Just a day."

A fresh torrent of rain battered the shelter. She imagined the tractibles squatting miserably in the open. Did tractibles experience misery? Did their sealed joints ache in the cold?

"Zoe, I have an alert here. We'll talk again."

Soon, she hoped. In the absence of his voice she felt doubly alone.

The squalls abated over the course of the day, followed by a cooling breeze from the west. Zoe had seen all sorts of Isian weather from the protected core of Yambuku, but you had to be outside—exposed—to appreciate the substance of the weather, its moods and subtleties.

Or maybe the failure of her thymostat had made her more sensitive.

More vulnerable.

Was this how the unregulated masses experienced the world? Everywhere she looked, Zoe seemed to find some shadow or echo of herself. In the tossing of the trees, the cascade of rainwater from leaf to leaf; in the cloudy daylight on the gorse, the sparkle of mica in ancient rocks. Mirrors.

We're not born with souls, Zoe thought; they invade us from outside, make themselves out of shadow and light, noon and midnight.

She wondered whether Theo had arrived from orbit yet, whether he was already deconning at Yambuku.

Did Theo have a soul? Had a soul ever colonized the perfect body of Avrion Theophilus?

She scouted her perimeter during the long afternoon, ranging within a kilometer of the digger colony, though she saw none of the animals. She avoided their foraging territory and their funerary grounds. She didn't want to alarm them; only, perhaps, leave a trace of her scent, a token of her presence.

She arrived back at camp well before sunset with her escort of spidery tractibles trailing behind her. The machines were mud-spattered and streaked with yellow pollen. One of them lagged badly. It had developed a limp.

Settled into her shelter for the night, she scrolled her own medical telemetry past her corneal display and requested an analgesic from the medical pack-mule to treat her various aches and itches.

High particulate content in the air—from forest fires in the far west—made the sunset long and gaudy. Zoe entered a few notes into her excursion log, made routine contact with Yambuku, and tried once more to sleep.

An alert roused her just past midnight. Tam's voice was in her ear as she sat up into the disorienting darkness: "Zoe?"

"Yes, I'm here, let me find a light—" She found and activated the tiny photostorage cell next to her bedroll. A "firefly lamp," they called it. About as bright.

Hayes went on, "We have major-malfunction tags on five of your tractibles—two of the packmules and three of the perimeter surveillors."

"Something attacked them?"

"Apparently just mechanical interrupts, but it can't be coincidental. I'm worried about the level of protection you're getting."

"Hardware malfs? You're sure?"

"Nuts-and-bolts failures."

"I'll fetch the repair kit and turn on some field lamps. Where are the tractibles now?"

"On your doorstep. We brought them in as soon as they began to complain. But, Zoe, we're getting strange telemetry from the remaining surveillors."

"Company?"

"Hard to say. Nothing big. We have remensors covering for the robots. But I want you to be careful."

The air outside was crisp and moist. A few stars adorned the sky. That nondescript one high in the northern quarter was Sol, if Zoe remembered her Isian constellations correctly. Cronos rode the hazy horizon.

Camp lights flared on, momentarily blinding her. She drew a deep breath. The filter of her excursion suit sterilized the ambient air but didn't warm it. A breath of Isis cooled her throat.

She retrieved a tool kit from one of the damaged pack-mule tractibles and scrolled the machine's telltales. Her corneal display listed multiple joint dysfunctions. A lubricant problem perhaps? She disassembled a ball-and-socket connector and found it fouled with what looked like mustard-yellow slime.

"Something got into the joint," she told Hayes. "Something biological. It must be eating the teflons."

There was no immediate answer. She wiped the joint clean with an absorbent cloth and locked it back into place. A temporary fix at best, but maybe she could patch one or two tractibles well enough to get herself and her essential equipment back to Yambuku. . . .

"Heads up, Zoe."

She looked up sharply.

The field lamps cast a searing white radiance all around her, a glow that faded into the dark of the forest beyond the meadow. She shaded her eyes and scanned the perimeter. Recognizable shapes began to disentangle themselves from the darkness.

Diggers had surrounded the clearing.

They stood at the perimeter of the meadow, spaced maybe five meters apart—twenty or more of them, some on four legs, some reared back on their hind pair. A few were armed with fire-hardened spears. Their black eyes glittered in the harsh light.

Her first reaction was fear. Her pulse ramped up and her palms began to sweat. These were animals, after all, like the lions she had once seen in a Trust preserve, but larger and vastly more strange. Cunning, unpredictable. The hint of intelligence that had made them seem so nearly human was less endearing in this windy darkness. There was intelligence here, certainly, but also a host of instincts purely Isian, purely unfathomable.

Thank God, they weren't advancing. Maybe the camp lights had attracted them. (Though what if those lights failed? What if a new set of malfunctions brought the full weight of the dark down on her?)

Or maybe these fears were a product of her thymostatic disorder. Systems failing inside and out, Zoe thought. But I was made for this. I was made for this. They're aware of me now, as I am aware of them. We see each other.

Hayes' voice erupted in her ear. "Stay still, Zoe, and we'll send one of the surviving tractibles into the forest, maybe draw their attention away from you. We have remensors nearby but the wind is making it hard to keep them airborne."

"No. No, Tam, don't."

"Excuse me?"

"They're not hostile."

"You can't know that."

"I'm not under attack. Something like this had to happen sooner or later."

"But not tonight. And you're coming home tomorrow."

"Tam, I may not get another chance. This is their first real-life encounter with a human being. Most likely they'll look me over for a while and just get bored. Keep the functioning tractibles ready, but don't make enemies."

"I'm not proposing to slaughter them, Zoe. Just—"

"Wait."

Movement on the perimeter. Zoe turned her head. One of the diggers had stepped out of rank. Its gait was two-legged, forelimbs raised, a fight-or-flight posture. It carried a sturdy branch in one hand. It stepped closer to the polyplex shelter, until Zoe recognized the array of white whiskers around the animal's muzzle. "It's Old Man!"

"Zoe—"

"Quiet!"

The moment was fragile. Zoe stood slowly from the place where she had crouched beside the tractible and took an infinitesimal step of her own toward Old Man. *What must he think I am? An animal, an enemy? A freakish reflection of himself?*

She held out her arms—empty hands, weaponless and clawless.

Hayes must have had at least one remensor nearby, because he had seen the motion too. "Three meters, Zoe. Closer than that, I herd him away. If any of the rest of them move, I want you next to the shelter, where we can protect you. Understand?"

She understood too much. She understood that she had reached her destiny point, that time and the circumstances of her life had conspired to bring her to this place. For one ecstatic moment she was the axis on which the stars revolved.

She took several bold steps forward. The digger reared up like a startled centipede. Its black eyes rolled in their sockets. Zoe slowed but didn't stop. She kept her hands in front of her, still a judicious distance from the animal.

But close enough to smell it. Close enough to see the steam rising from its warm underbelly into the night air. Four billion years of un-Earthly evolution had shaped this aggregate of cells, this beast. She looked at it. And, amazingly, it looked at her. An impossible distance from the planet of her birth, this miracle had happened: Clay had made life. Life regarded life. *First light,* Zoe thought.

The digger was very quick. It drew back the tree branch it was hefting before Zoe could begin to flinch.

No, not like this, she thought. *It shouldn't be like this—*

"Zoe?"

Hayes' voice was distant and irrelevant.

No time to step back, take shelter behind the tractibles. The tractibles had begun to move, but slowly. *More systems failing?* The digger raised its left upper forearm, the club secure in its gripping hand. She saw the downward swing of it with frozen clarity.

The impact blurred everything. She fell through the windy night.

SIXTEEN

ALTHOUGH HE HAD prayed he would never have to do it, containing biological contamination aboard the Isis Orbital Station was the first task for which Kenyon Degrandpre had been trained. The crisis and its thousand details occupied all his attention. And that was infinitely better than allowing himself to consider the long-term consequences of the outbreak.

He summoned all five of the station's senior managers, including Leander of Medical (replacing the quarantined Corbus Nefford) and Sullivan of Foodstuffs and Biota. They were a motley collation of Trust outriders—all of them competent managers, none of them Family except by the most distant and tenuous connection. Degrandpre himself had such a connection; his maternal great-grandfather had been a Corbille. But the birth was unregistered and hence irrelevant.

His first order of business had been to contain the quarantine pod, and he had done that. Before today the IOS had been a sterile zone, isolated from Isis by the hard vacuum beyond its walls. Now the IOS was itself a breached environment, an apple into which a dangerous worm had gnawed.

The isolation ward had become a Level Five hot zone, contained on its perimeter by fiat Level Four zones—these were the exterior medical chambers, such as the one in which Corbus Nefford was currently trapped—and by Level One, Two, and Three precautionary zones beyond that, i.e., the engineering pod and a maintenance space where Turing assemblers were prepared for launch.

The problem was, there was very little redundancy aboard the IOS. The size and weight restrictions imposed by the mechanics of the Higgs launches narrowed the margin of error to a fine line. Even at peak efficiency, the IOS had always been one or two critical failures away from wholesale shutdown. Without the machine shop, and with access restricted to the Turing launchers—

But no; that was tomorrow's problem.

Solen of Engineering said, "We're looking at how to relocate critical functions as far as possible from the hot pod. The farms, thank God, are about as far from quarantine as you can get, a hundred eighty degrees of the circle. We're setting up a temporary clinic for injuries outside the agriculture perimeter; disease cases, if any, go directly to the quarantine perimeter."

Degrandpre pictured the IOS in his mind, a necklace of ten gray pearls spinning in a void. No, nine gray pearls and one black: infected, infectious. He would have to move his own quarters closer to the farms.

Certainly the new Turing gens would have to wait; it meant another delay for the D&P interferometer project, but that was unavoidable. The grand plan to use Isis as a staging base for further Higgs launches depended on a stable Isian outpost—to be defended at all costs. Without the IOS, Degrandpre thought, the Trusts will lose the stars, at least for the foreseeable future.

His most immediate problem, though, was not contagion, but fear. The fact of the outbreak in Quarantine could hardly be hidden from the fifteen-hundred-plus crew of the orbital station, each of whom was painfully aware of being locked in a metal canister without plausible hope of escape. An emergency Higgs launch, Solen told him blandly, would save ten or twelve people depending on their combined mass.

"Motivate your workers," Degrandpre said, "but don't terrify them. Emphasize that these are extraordinary precautions we're taking, that there has been no contamination outside the quarantine chamber."

Leander of Medical said, "They know that, Manager, but they also have the example of the ground stations before them. The suspicion is that once contamination occurs, there's no certain way to contain it."

"Tell them we're talking about one organism here, not the whole Isian biosphere."

"One organism? Is that true?"

"Possibly. Keeping order is more important than telling the truth."

The meeting moved on briskly, working through Degrandpre's prepared agenda. So far, so good: the contagion had been contained, food and water supplies were safe, and other essential functions remained in good shape. The IOS was still a safe environment.

What had been stolen from them by the event in Quarantine was their sense of security. We have always been fragile, Degrandpre thought. But never as fragile as now.

Degrandpre ordered his communications manager to stay behind when the others left.

"I want all outbound messages routed through my office for approval, including routine housekeeping. Let's not alarm the Trusts prematurely."

The communications manager, a bony Terrestrial woman named Nakamura, shifted her weight uncomfortably. "That's highly unusual," she said—letting him know, Degrandpre supposed, that she wouldn't cover for him if the Trusts eventually brought a complaint.

Young woman, he thought, that is the least of your problems. He noted her objection and dismissed her.

There was nothing here the Families needed to know, at least not right away. Above all else, the Trusts feared the consequences of importing an Isian pathogen to Earth. Alarm them, and the Trusts might well impose an extended quarantine . . . or even refuse to dock a Higgs module returned from Isis, leaving the survivors to drift until they starved.

Degrandpre didn't relish the prospect of becoming one more frozen planetisimal, entombed in a sort of artificial Kuiper body, a cometary mausoleum arcing through endless orbits of the sun.

He spoke to Corbus Nefford through a video link.

The station's chief physician was clearly frightened. His uniform was ringed with perspiration; his face was pale and doughy, his eyes perpetually too wide. Degrandpre imagined the man's thymostat pressed to its limits, synthesizing regulatory molecules at a feverish pitch.

"It's absurd," Nefford insisted, "at a time like this, that I should be *confined* here . . ."

"I don't doubt it, Corbus. But that's the way the containment protocols are written."

"Written by pedantic theorists who obviously don't understand—"

"Written by the Trusts. Watch your language, Doctor."

Nefford's narrow eyebrows and small mouth contracted petulantly, as if, Degrandpre thought, someone had tightened his stitches. The station's former managing physician seemed on the verge of tears, not a good omen. "You don't understand. These people died so *quickly.*"

"They died in Quarantine, yes?"

"Yes, but—"

"Then you should be safe enough."

"All I want is to put some distance between myself and the

contamination. Is that so unreasonable? Everyone else is huddling near the gardens, I understand. Why should I be used this way?"

"It's not your decision, Doctor."

"I've worked in clean environments all my life. I'm a Family physician! I maintain health! I don't perform autopsies! I'm not accustomed to this degree of, of . . ."

Nefford trailed off, swiping his forehead on his sleeve. The managing physician was sick.

With fear.

Let it be fear, Degrandpre thought. For once, he envied his father's stubborn faith. A prophet to pray to. Here, there was no prophet, no Mecca, no Jerusalem. No paradise or forgiveness, no margin of error. Only a devil. And the devil was fecund, the devil was alive.

SEVENTEEN

THE EVACUATION OF Marburg took a day and a half.

The field station was a twin of Yambuku, set deep in the Lesser Boreal Continent's temperate forest. Like Yambuku, it was situated in a cleared perimeter, its rigorously sterile core contained inside layers of increasing biohazard. Its biologically hot outer walls were scrubbed daily by maintenance tractibles, or should have been—lately the tractibles had begun to malfunction; the bays were full of machinery demanding maintenance, and bacterial films had compromised three of the station's exit locks. When the shuttle dock seals began to show similar wear, the station manager, a Shoe Clan virologist named Weber, called for general evac.

The call was not well-received by the IOS. Apparently Marburg's shuttle would be routed to a secondary bay that was being set up for prolonged quarantine. Weber ascribed this to Terrestrial paranoia, though he feared it might signal something worse.

But there was no postponing the evac. Weber loved Isis and

had worked hard to make Marburg a going concern. But he was also a realist. Postpone the evacuation much longer and people would begin to die.

The Oceanic Station had already collapsed. The Isis Polar Station, anchored in the glacial wasteland of the planet's northern ice cap, reported no significant problems and continued to operate on a day-to-day basis.

Yambuku, however, was on the brink of total breakdown.

Avrion Theophilus burst through the shuttle-bay doors from de-con, brushed aside his courtesy detail, and marched directly to Yambuku's remote-ops room.

His full-dress Devices and Personnel uniform drew a few stares from the otherwise distracted downstation crew. He was accustomed to that, at least from the Kuiper-born. In civilization it would have been considered ridiculously gauche, the peasant's impulse to stare. But Yambuku wasn't civilization.

He found the station manager, Tam Hayes, coming off a long remensor session. Hayes looked groggy, unshaven. Theophilus took him aside. "We need a place to talk."

"I gather she's injured," Theophilus said.

"It looks that way."

"Out of contact."

"Verbal contact, certainly. We're still getting some telemetry, but it's intermittent. The fault may be with our antenna array. Remensors are down, too, and the excursion tractibles are dead. All of them."

"But Zoe is not."

"No. To the best of our knowledge, Zoe is not."

"We have good telemetry up to the point at which she was attacked?"

"Yes."

"Forwarded to Earth?"

"Forwarded to the IOS, at least. Degrandpre bottlenecks traffic to Earth."

"I wouldn't worry about that."

Hayes blinked. "Believe me, that's not what I'm worried about."

"Have the satellites located her?"

"To within a meter of the digger colony, but the atmosphere's too cloudy for any kind of visual confirmation."

"Not good enough," Theophilus said.

They had come to the small shuttle-control chamber above the core. It was occupied only during launches—a good place for a private conversation. Hayes was in a hurry to get back to the remote-ops room; Zoe was alive, and he meant to bring her back to Yambuku. Right now Avrion Theophilus was only an obstacle, and the man's peremptory manner made Hayes clench his fists.

He said, "Are you worried about Zoe or about her excursion technology?"

"The technology has already proven itself, don't you think? The fact that she might yet be alive despite a wild-animal attack is evidence of that."

"Because if it's Zoe you're worried about, it might be best if you let me get back to the business of bringing her home."

"Not all the novel technology is in her excursion suit, Dr. Hayes."

"Excuse me?"

"She's a package. It isn't just the interface. She's augmented *internally*, do you understand? She has an entirely artificial immune system riding on top of her natural immunity. Microscopic nano-factories stapled to her abdominal aorta. If the suit is breached, we need to know that. There's much more we can learn from her even if she dies in the field."

"You're saying she might survive even if the suit is breached?"

"For a time, at least. It might be difficult to retrieve her body, given the situation here. But if we can—"

"Fuck you," Hayes said.

He didn't want to retrieve Zoe's body. He had a better plan.

Dieter Franklin came into the staging bay as Hayes was suiting up.

Hayes' standard bioarmor was clumsy and immense compared to the gear Zoe had worn. A sterile core wrapped in steel and flexiglass and nanofilters. Hayes had just sealed the massive leggings when the inner door slid open.

"You can't be serious," Franklin said. "Lee Reisman said you were raving about an emergency excursion. I told her you were smarter than that. Tell me I wasn't lying."

"I'm bringing her back."

"Slow down a fucking minute and think about this! You're planning to cross the Copper River in a suit of armor that can sustain you for, what, two days maximum?—when it's working properly. And at a time when every piece of machinery we've sent into the field is either dead or failing and we can't even keep our own seals intact."

"She's alive, maybe injured."

"If she's alive, she needs a functioning ground station to come home to. You're more useful to her here. Not out in the mud with a hot servomotor, or worse, dividing everybody's attention and costing us resources we can't afford."

"I owe her—"

"Nothing you owe her is worth suicide. And that's what this is, you *know* it. Odds are, you'll end up as a few kilograms of compost inside a broken steel shell. And Zoe will end up right where she is."

Hayes wound a layer of insulation around his waist, forcing himself to slow down, do it right. "She was a fucking *test platform*, Dieter. D-and-P doesn't give a shit about the diggers. Zoe thought she was here to do social studies, but she was a *test platform*."

Dieter Franklin nodded slowly. "For the excursion suit. Elam suspected as much."

"Elam suspected. But I *knew.*"

Franklin said nothing. Hayes tried to focus his attention on his armor, working the procedures, sealing bands of pneumostatic plastic over his rib cage. He wished Elam were here to read him his checklist.

"You *knew?*"

"I saw all the D-and-P memos. Little communiqués to the Yambuku manager. No details, but enough that I should have realized it was her gear that mattered. She was a fucking test platform, Dieter, and I let her walk out there in all her glorious ignorance."

"You need to think about this. She has good gear, but it's not breach-proof. We can't be sure she's still alive."

Next, the soft inner helmet. "She has more than the suit. She's been internally modified. She has a heavily augmented immune system. Even if her suit's damaged, she might survive long enough for us to get her back here. Maybe long enough to save her life."

Dieter Franklin was silent for a time.

He said at last, "Even so, Tam. It's a bad bet."

"I know it's a bad bet."

"Because Yambuku won't *be* here much longer. That's the obvious conclusion no one wants to draw. Look at the Oceanic Station. Look at Marburg. It's the bios, Tam, working out strategies, learning how to corrupt our seals and our locks. Synthesizing solvents and spreading the knowledge, *sharing* it somehow. Five years ago, that biohazard armor was good enough to protect you. Today . . . it's the next best thing to fucking useless."

Hayes toggled the atmosphere lock. Overhead, a series of fans began to create positive pressure. An alarm sounded. Dieter Franklin fled the room.

Hayes pulled on his helmet.

EIGHTEEN

P AIN. DOUBLE VISION. Zoe felt herself being dragged, the heels of her boots bumping against impediments. She was suffering from concussion, she thought vaguely, or worse, from some cranial injury from which she wouldn't recover. She smelled impossible things: burning rubber, ammonia, rotting food; and when she closed her eyes she saw pinwheels and flares.

She was terribly nauseated but dared not vomit. The excursion suit would process the mess, but probably not before she choked to death.

She was awake, or perhaps not: consciousness ebbed; time passed in gusts, like the wind.

S he struggled—briefly—when she realized the diggers were dragging her into one of their mounds, away from starlight and firelight and into the rocky, claustrophobic dark.

The mound entrance was narrow. The diggers spindled their

sickeningly mobile bodies and entered one at a time; Zoe was dragged by her extended arms, helpless, over the rocky lip and into a tunnel encrusted with digger excretions. The air was thick with an unfamiliar stench, spicy and foul at once, like cardamom and rotted food. She wondered if she would asphyxiate here. In the dark.

And for the first time in her life, Zoe felt panic.

She had not panicked even in the cold dormitories of the orphan crib; her thymostat had suppressed any violent emotion and left only a hollow, pervasive sadness, the aching knowledge of her captivity and abandonment. What she felt now was worse. There was no advantage to struggle but she felt she *must* struggle. The need to fight obliterated thought, became a madness rising out of the meat of her. She tried to suppress the scream that rose from her chest but the effort was futile; the scream erupted and continued without reason or volition. She kicked and pulled at the coral-sharp claws that held her wrists and ankles. But these animals were complacently strong. All light vanished. There was only darkness now, and compulsive motion, and the enclosing walls of the tunnel. And the sound of her sobbing.

She woke again—alone, exhausted beyond fear.

Was she blind? No. It was only the darkness of the diggers' mound. Aboveground it might be noon or midnight. Here, it was always dark.

But at least she was alone, at least for now. She moved, stretched tentatively . . . found a rocky ceiling just above her head, too close to allow her to stand, curving to arm's-length walls and a floor somehow softer (but damper) than the entrance tunnel had been. The silence beat at her ears. The only audible sounds were the rattle of her breath inside the suit's filter and the rasp of her movements. If she had a light—

But she did! She did have a light. Several, in fact: the firefly lamps strapped to her tool belt, the tool belt she had been using to mend the tractibles.

Stupid, stupid, languishing in the blackness when she could have been *seeing!* She fumbled at her belt almost fearfully, and indeed some of the small lamps had torn away during her struggle, but some of them remained, as small as bullets and with an activator built into each base. She extracted one and thumbed its switch.

The light it emitted was faint but welcome. Order was restored; she was in a place with contours and dimensions—a rounded pressed-earth hollow glistening with damp. The floor was carpeted with a pale, almost translucent growth through which small mandibled insects crawled, and on the wall there was the gauzy nest of some spider-like creature, a mass of cotton-floss thread to which the mummified bodies of insects adhered.

The firefly lamp was good for an hour or two. There were seven more remaining on her belt; she counted them with her fingers. She would have to be careful.

But of course she couldn't stay here. She couldn't even if she wanted to. No food. No water. She had some water reserves in her suit, which would recycle her urine, too, but that was an open loop and good for maybe a day or two at most without exterior replenishment. Basically, she needed to get to her base camp, find food and water and maybe a working tractible, then head back to Yambuku.

Resources, Zoe thought. She was perhaps not thinking very clearly; her head ached horribly where the digger had clubbed her, and when she touched her temple she felt a plump bruise under the excursion suit's membrane. Resources: what did she have that she could use to her advantage? Telemetry, communication . . . the thought of talking to Tam Hayes was so enticing she almost wept. But when she called up her coms protocol there was no carrier— nothing from Yambuku, wide- or narrow-band, which meant that her gear was damaged, or *theirs* was, or perhaps the digger mound was blocking radio transmissions.

She wondered then how far below the surface she had been carried. She didn't know—no one knew—how deep these tunnels ran. There had been a few seismic-imaging experiments conducted by remotely operated tractibles near the digger mounds, enough to

suggest that the warrens were extensive and complexly intercon-
nected. The digging might have gone on for centuries, might have
reached down kilometers below the topsoil. . . . But no, that was
a bad thought. Impermissible. She felt panic rising like a lump in
her throat. Daylight might be a kilometer away, but it also might
be just an inch above this sealed chamber. She had no way of
knowing and she instructed herself not to think about it.

She held her breath for a moment and listened carefully. Was
she alone? A tunnel roughly as wide as her shoulders was the only
entrance to this cul-de-sac. The firefly lamp would not illuminate
that space beyond a meter or so; she saw only that the tunnel was
circular and that it rose at a gentle angle, perhaps twenty degrees
of slope. *Listen.* She held herself still and tried to calm the pulsing
of blood in her ears. *Listen.* But the silence was absolute. Surely a
digger traversing these tunnels would betray itself by the sound of
its passage, claws on soil packed as hard as rock. There was no such
sound. Good.

Maybe it was daytime, Zoe thought, and the diggers were outside gathering food. She tried to scroll a clock, but her corneal
display seemed to be broken. Another effect of the blow to her
head perhaps.

She hesitated for what might have been a moment or an hour,
eyeing the crawl space suspiciously, reluctant to exchange this relatively spacious cell for the cramped enclosure of the tunnel. But
then the firefly lamp began to sputter and dim, and anything, Zoe
thought, *anything* would be better than more darkness.

She plucked another lamp from her belt and struck it, but it
wouldn't light. It was broken.

Her fingers shook as she worked the next lamp free. This one,
when she pressed it, sprang brightly to life. She sighed her relief.

But that left only five more lamps . . . and none or all of them
might have gone bad.

Now, Zoe, she thought. Go now.

She held the firefly lamp in her right hand and lay down on
her stomach. The albino moss felt cool beneath her suit membrane.
She would have to advance with her arms in front of her, squirming

more than crawling, using her boots for traction. And what if she
lost herself in this maze? What if all her firefly lamps burned out,
one by one? Could she even take another one from her belt in
such a narrow space?

No, she realized, not without dislocating her shoulder.

She backed off, removed her tool belt and slipped it over one
shoulder. That way she could reach the remaining lamps, if need
be.

Five lamps. Say, six or seven hours of light, if they all worked.
And then—?

Another bad thought. She put it out of her mind and squirmed
once more into the tunnel.

There was just enough space for her to lift herself on her elbows
and inch forward, scrabbling with boots and knees in a sort of crab-
crawl. She was grateful for the ubiquitous pale moss beneath her;
it cushioned her knees and elbows where the vulnerable suit
membrane might have torn or eroded.

The firefly lamp illuminated a narrow circular space perhaps a
meter or two ahead of her. I need a plan, she thought. (Perhaps
she said some of this aloud. She tried not to, but the gap between
thought and word had narrowed and she caught the occasional
echo of her own hoarse whisper coming back to her out of the
distance. Giving herself away, she feared. But still, the animals
hadn't returned.)

A plan, she thought again. Here was a maze, and somewhere
the minotaur. She decided that whenever she came to a fork in the
tunnel she would always take the path that led upward, or if both
paths were equivalent she would take the right-turning branch.
That way she would eventually reach the surface, or at least be able
(but please don't let it happen) to back out of a dead end and retrace
her route.

She could do that, she decided, even if, God forbid, she used
up all her lamps. Even in the dark, she could do that.

The dark returned when her current lamp flickered and
dimmed. Too soon, surely. How far had she come? She couldn't
guess. A long way, it seemed, but not far enough. The tunnel had

not branched, not even once. Or perhaps, horrible thought, the diggers made new tunnels and sealed old ones; maybe she would reach a final wall and—

No. *Bad* thought.

She fumbled another firefly lamp into her hand and pressed the base. To her immense relief, it flickered to life.

Another hour lost.

Bad thought, bad thought.

She had been imagining, vividly, what she would do when she got back to Yambuku—peel off her excursion membrane, stand under a hot shower, wash her hair, eat, drink sparkling water from tall crystal tumblers—when she came to a branching tunnel.

The first. Or was it the first? Here in this small arc of light it was hard to estimate time, to distinguish between events imagined and events actual. She had planned this, but had she already attempted it? She didn't know. Nevertheless, Zoe thought, stick to plan. Did the left branch show an upward slope, or should she keep to the right?

Hard to say.

She paused, hoping to divine some clue. Was there a breath of wind either way? There was not. Only the same stale, stinking air, hardly enough to fill her lungs. No sound. She thought perhaps the right-hand tunnel rose ever so slightly, and she turned in that direction.

Running into Theo's arms.

"One of my children survived."

Running into Tam Hayes' arms. . . .

She woke hurting. Arms stiff, legs stiff, her head throbbing. Pressure all around her. And blind—

No, it was the dark.

The dark.

She had fallen asleep.

She cursed her carelessness—time had been wasted!—and fumbled for the next firefly lamp. She kept her eyes tightly closed as she worked her fingers, because she couldn't see anything even if her eyes were open, and because with her eyes closed the darkness felt like a choice, her own chosen darkness, not something imposed by the weight of clay and stone around her. The warm darkness, perhaps, of sleep. Though she must *not* sleep again.

She scratched the lamp alight.

That was better. Only this endless tunnel to see, but the light was a blessing.

She crawled ahead a few meters—or maybe a lot of meters. There were no references here any longer, no time and no space. She might have traveled a great distance already, or she might be a scant few paces from her original cul-de-sac.

Bad thought.

The tunnel ahead of her began to widen. This was change at last, and the rush of hope she felt was intoxicating. She cautioned herself against it, but hope was like panic, irrepressible, a vast force no longer blocked by her thymostat.

The thymostat had been a kind of membrane too, Zoe thought like her excursion suit, another barrier between herself and the world. Shutting out the viruses of panic and hope and love and despair. Lost now. She was naked and infected.

The tunnel continued to expand, became a larger chamber. She filled it with the sound of her labored breathing. Raised her hand and brought the light to bear. Lifted her eyes and saw—

—a dead end.

Another cul-de-sac.

She let her tears flow freely for a few precious minutes. The excursion suit, she thought idiotically, would recycle them.

She crawled back, sobbing intermittently, to the place where the tunnel branched.

How many lamps were left? Her memory was faulty; she was compelled to stop and count the remaining lamps with her fingers. One, two, three, four. Which meant that hours had passed since she left the chamber where she had been abandoned. She could even calculate the time, she supposed, if her mind were functioning a little more efficiently, if she had not lost an eternity to sleep.

Too much time, in any case. Too much time spent doubling her tracks.

She thought of open air. The memory was so vivid she could taste it. And sky, Zoe thought. Yes, and rain. And wind.

She heard faint sounds at the tunnel intersection. An exit missed? The sound of *outside?* But she had to be careful. She controlled her breathing. She put her head into the adjoining tunnel.

Where the black eyes of a digger regarded her coolly.

She held on to the firefly lamp even as the digger scuttled after her and clutched her ankles.

She hadn't recognized the digger. It wasn't Old Man. Absurd as that name was. This was simply an animal, or something as much insect as animal, long and too lithe in the close confinement of the tunnel, its thin body flexible, huge black eyes queasily mobile in their sockets, gripping claws tight as rings of tempered steel. She was shocked that she had ever found anything even faintly reminiscent of the human about these creatures. They were brutal but not even malevolent; their minds worked in strange, inhuman loops; whatever motivated them, she was opaque to it; their realm was not her realm.

It dragged her into another cul-de-sac—no, oh God, the *same* one, the one she had started from; she recognized the web on the wall—and rolled her over on her back.

Still she clutched the lamp. A small spark of sanity. The digger ignored it.

She closed her eyes, opened them.

The digger loomed over her. She supposed it was looking at her, though its eyes were as blank as bubbles of oil.

She looked back at it. Beneath her panic was a grim and wholly unexpected calm, an emotional deadness that was both relief and threat at once. A *premature* deadness . . . because she was almost certainly about to die.

The digger put one extended claw on her chest, on her sternum above her breasts.

She felt the pressure of it—enough to cause pain, perhaps enough to draw blood.

Then the digger began to slice at her excursion membrane, peeling away the broken material like pale, dead skin.

NINETEEN

ALL ROADS LEAD to Rome, Kenyon Degrandpre thought, and out here at the edge of the human diaspora he had become the embodiment of Rome, and down those roads marched all the bad news in the world, rank on serried rank.

Each new crisis demanded a fresh solution. The written emergency protocols had proved woefully inadequate.

The evacuation of Marburg, for instance. Clearly, the station manager was justified in calling the evac. Just as clearly, Degrandpre couldn't sacrifice much more of the limited space aboard the IOS for a lengthy quarantine of fifteen individuals, any of whom might be vectoring some virulent microorganism. He resolved the conflict by housing the Marburg evacuees in a vacant engineering bay ordinarily used to launch Turing assemblers. Crude, cold, and uncomfortable quarters, but he ordered the chamber stocked with a week's worth of food and water and equipped with sleeping mats, and considered himself generous for so doing. He also ordered the access doors double-sealed and declared the bay a Level Five hot zone pro tem.

And in his rare free moments—the calm, he imagined, of a falling object, a crystal goblet dropped from a tray before it strikes the floor—he was obliged to shuffle through routine Earth-bound particle-pair traffic to ensure that no hint of the ongoing crisis reached the wrong ears.

This paranoiac rant, for instance, from Yambuku's resident planetologist, Dieter Franklin:

> Mounting evidence suggests a mechanism of information exchange between physically unconnected living cells. Such a mechanism would allow a symbiosis that rides above the usual evolutionary process, a mechanism perhaps as significant as the ancient Terrestrial symbiosis of unicellular life and primitive mitochondria. . . .

Whatever that meant.

> The increasing efficiency of bacteriological attack on downstation seals and the penetration of supposedly inert barriers (a phenomenon shared across immense distances by otherwise unrelated organisms) led to the investigation of intracellular quantum events such as . . .

No, strike all that. "Bacterial attack" would raise an alarm back home. Feeling faintly guilty, but with the clinical determination of a man who has set about the grim task of ensuring his own survival, Degrandpre deleted the offending paragraph.

> The proliferation of structurally unnecessary microtubules in a great variety of Isian unicells may ultimately explain this apparent action-at-a-distance. In the human brain, such structures mediate consciousness by operating as quantum devices, a single electron's indeterminacy amplified, in effect, to

become the central mechanism of vertebrate consciousness. Preliminary laboratory work (see appendix) suggests that Isian unicells not only sustain a similar quantum effect but can in fact create and preserve twin-state particle-pair coherency during the process of mitosis.

All this seemed wrongheaded and subtly threatening to Degrandpre, though he was hardly equipped to evaluate the scientific content. He skipped to the summary at the end of the document:

One may speculate, perhaps not prematurely, about the possibilities inherent in a pseudoneural network connecting all Isian unicells, a biomass that (if one includes oceanic matter and the mineral-fixing bacteria distributed through the crust of the planet) is of truly staggering proportions. The increasingly successful biological attacks on the downstations might be seen by analogy as an autonomic reaction to the presence of a foreign body, in which breach strategies developed in the saline environment of the ocean and first used against the oceanic research station were slowly but effectively adapted for use against land-based outposts. . . .

No, none of this would do.

An incoming message chimed his scroll—tagged Highest Priority, of course; what else? Degrandpre ordered a quick global delete of the floating document. Dieter Franklin's musings were promptly excised from the scroll, the mail queue, and the central memory. They would not, of course, be broadcast to Earth.

The bad news this time—and it was very bad news indeed—was that Corbus Nefford had developed a fever.

Degrandpre spoke to his medical manager through a two-way screen, full-scale image. Under the circumstances, a scroll connection would have been too formal. Never mind that he spoke from the safety of his temporary command quarters, lodged next to the aeroponic gardens. Never mind that he had already established four new precautionary zones, extending from the shuttle dock to include both adjoining pods and, of course, the Turing launch bays.

He was shocked at the sight of Corbus Nefford strapped to a gurney with a saline drip tacked to his arm and Ken Kinsolving at his side. Remote tractibles bustled around the physician's bedside, snuffling at his wrists with biotic and chemical sensors. Nefford had insisted he had something important to tell Kenyon Degrandpre and had refused to speak to intermediates. At the moment he looked barely capable of speaking at all.

We are all lost, some part of Degrandpre whispered.

He mustered his diplomatic skills. He didn't want Nefford to see him flinch away from the screen.

"What you have to understand," Nefford managed to gasp, "is the *slowness* of it. . . ."

The etiology of the disease, or Nefford's own death? Each protracted; each agonizing. "Yes, go on," Degrandpre said. All of this was being recorded by the IOS's central memory for future reference. He wondered whether anyone would ever see it.

"This disease isn't like other Isian contagions. Not as virulent. It has an incubation period. That means it's probably a single organism. Dangerous and subtle, but potentially controllable. Do you understand?"

"I understand. You needn't continue asking me that, Corbus."

"Dangerous, but potentially controllable. But quarantine isn't working. We're dealing with something very small here, maybe a prion, a bit of DNA in a protein jacket, maybe small enough to tunnel through the seals. . . ."

"We'll keep all that in mind, Corbus." *If any of us survive.*

"Manager," Nefford gasped, his mouth working between syllables like a siphon with an air bubble trapped inside. "May I say 'Kenyon'? We're friends, aren't we? In keeping with our respective positions in the Trust?"

Hardly.

"Of course," Degrandpre said.

"Maybe I won't die."

"Perhaps not."

"We can control this."

"Yes," Degrandpre said.

Nefford seemed on the verge of saying something more. But fresh red blood began to leak from his nose. Visibly disappointed, he closed his eyes and turned his head away. Kinsolving broke the video connection.

"Ghastly," Degrandpre murmured. He couldn't seem to escape the word. It was lodged on his tongue. "Ghastly. Ghastly."

Nefford's prophecy was correct. Engineering tractibles reported microscopic pinhole punctures in the seals separating the original quarantine chamber from the surrounding quarters.

Here was the real horror, Degrandpre thought, this breaking of barriers. Civilization, after all, was the making of divisions, of walls and fences to parse the chaotic wild into ordered cells of human imagination. Wilderness invades the garden and reason is overthrown.

He understood for the first time, or imagined he understood, his father's religious impulse. The Families and their Trusts had finely divided and obsessively ordered the political and technological wilderness of Earth, each person and thing and process in its appropriate orbit in the social orrery; but outside the walls of the Families the wild still pressed close: proles, Martians, Kuiper clans; disease vectors breeding in the haunts of the underclasses; no conqueror but death, finally, and the cruel immensity of the universe. His father's furtive Islam was, after all, an act of will, the ordering of the void into story and hierarchy, walled gardens of good and evil.

The tragedy of Isis was the tragedy of walls made vain. Not only the physical walls. He thought of Corbus Nefford calling him a "friend." He thought of the hygienic lies he broadcast to Earth on a daily basis.

All vain. Very little could be salvaged now. Perhaps only his own life. Perhaps not even that.

A summit with the pompous, fat chief engineer, Todd Solen.

"As I see it," Solen announced, "we have just one recourse. If we can't put physical barriers between ourselves and the disease agent, whatever it is, we have to shut down Modules Three and Six, secure the bulkheads, and evacuate the atmosphere. Put a sector of hard vacuum between ourselves and the threat. Which ought to do the trick, unless this so-called virus has spread through the IOS already."

"The Marburg evacuees are in Module Six."

"Obviously. They'll die if we depressurize the module. But they'll die just as surely if we don't. Disease aside, without access to our Turing bays or main shuttle docks, without spares or a comprehensive engineering sector, with our water circulation compromised and the food supply dependening entirely on what we can grow in the sun gardens—all considered, the IOS is an unsustainable environment. We can save as many people as we can fit into a single Higgs launcher. No more."

Degrandpre felt the paralysis of utter failure.

He asked, "Has it come to that?"

The engineer was perspiring freely. He swabbed his forehead with a sleeve. "With all due respect, Manager, yes, it has come to that."

I will not render this decision, Degrandpre thought, under intimidation. He said, "It's hot in here."

Solen blinked his bulging eyes. "Well—we're recycling water from the cooling fins. There's not much left for thermostatic control."

"Find a way to make it cooler in here, Mr. Solen."

"Yes, sir," Solen said faintly.

Too hot, too dry. The IOS itself was running a fever.

.   .   .

Aaron Weber, the Marburg station manager currently isolated in the Turing bay—along with all fifteen of his staff—also took note of the heat.

The air was dry, enervating, and it made even the large if poorly illuminated steel cavern of the Turing bay seem claustrophobic.

Sleep proved difficult in the heat. The heat dried throat and nose, made clothing a nuisance and blankets intolerable. Several of the Kuiper-born scientists stripped and thought nothing of it, but Weber was more inhibited. He was reminded of his student dormitory in Kim Il Sung City during the long winters, blistering forced-air heat losing its moisture to glass windows crusted with ice. Nosebleeds at night, bloodstains on the pillow. The only recourse had been to open a window and risk freezing.

Fully clothed, he nevertheless managed to sleep for an hour or so in the long shadow of a cargo manipulator, woke to the snoring of his quarantined comrades, slept again. . . .

And woke with a faint, cool breeze on his cheek.

Thinking of the dormitory window. Snow sliding under glass. The moving air soothed him.

But the air here ought not to be moving.

The breeze became a wind now, a brisk little indoor wind sweeping along the floor of the Turing bay with surprising vigor, picking up loose items rescued from the shuttle: here a foam cup, there a sheaf of printed paper.

He sat upright, alarmed.

That sound? That muted throbbing? He recognized it from the IOS launches, though it had never been so immediate: it was the sound of the machinery that opened the bay's huge airlock.

His ears exploded with pain as the atmospheric pressure abruptly dropped. When he opened his mouth the air spilled out of his throat in an involuntary exhalation that seemed never to end. He wanted to cry out, but his lungs collapsed like broken balloons.

Lights blinked out around him. He saw bodies thrashing as they were thrown from the gaping lock. No noise now. Only the stars, pure and unmediated. The fixed and naked eye. First light.

TWENTY

YESTERDAY'S RAINWATER DRIPPED from the forest canopy and left the trail mulchy and slick. Tam Hayes moved
cautiously in his heavy biological armor. He had grown
accustomed to the liquid sound of his footsteps in the decaying
biomass, the regular whir of his servomotors. The sounds were
peaceful, in a strange way.

Throughout that long day he did not speak to Yambuku, although message alerts scrolled periodically through his heads-up.
The silence was oddly soothing. Instead, he performed the slow
and steady work of navigating his armor, pacing himself, monitoring his gear. He wanted to reach and preferably cross the Copper
River by nightfall. If necessary he would sleep inside his armor,
simply freeze the servos and let the gel padding accommodate itself
to his weight. But it would be better to keep moving. Dieter had
been right, of course, about the bioarmor. He dared not depend
on it. It would fail—in some small way or catastrophically; sooner
or later.

Much as he tried to pace himself, however, this was hard physical labor. The sweat poured out of him, some of it absorbed by the armor's recyclers but most of it trapped between his body and the cool gel membrane, irritating his skin. He watched his footing as he walked, avoiding places where the mud seemed threateningly deep. He saw the sky reflected in leaf-strewn puddles, sunlight glistening on scummy water.

And it occurred to him to wonder, from time to time, what he was doing out here.

Searching for Zoe, of course, because he cared about Zoe. She was fragile but brutally persistent—he thought for a moment of a fern emerging from a poisonous windfall of volcanic ash. She had been subjected to cruelties that had killed four of her clone sisters, and she had survived—had followed Isis out of her captivity, just as Hayes had followed Isis away from his family and his clan.

But we were both seduced, Hayes thought.

Would Zoe have come here so willingly if she had known she was nothing more than a vehicle for the field testing of new Trust technologies? God help us, Hayes thought, she might have; but the Trust never offered her the choice. Lies wrapped in lies, everyone a party to some sin or other; knowledge hoarded and tightly held, because knowledge was power. The Terrestrial way.

And I am out here, Hayes thought, out here in this peaceful toxic wilderness, to rescue her . . . but admit the truth: to rescue himself as well.

The awful thing about lying was that it became a habit, then a reflex, as automatic as the blinking of the eyes or the voiding of the bowels. Lying was the Terrestrial disease, his mother used to say. Calm, aloof, an Ice Walker, his father's potlatch wife. In some other century she might have been a Quaker.

He had wanted the stars but he had caught the Terrestrial disease, the unknowing of awkward truths.

He had lied to Zoe. Perhaps not as egregiously as Avrion Theophilus had lied to her—but he had abetted those lies.

He was out here saving Zoe, but he was also out here salvaging the tattered remains of his innocence. No points for that.

.   .   .

He reached the river at sunset. The sky was clean, deepening toward indigo, and the small moon was quartered at zenith. He wanted to cross the river before dark.

The recent rains had swollen the Copper. Water surged over the surface of the crude bridge the tractibles had built. Hayes stepped onto that fragile scaffolding and felt it sway beneath his weight. If the bridge collapsed, he would be trapped beneath the running water by the unbuoyant mass of his armor.

He switched on his helmet lamp and advanced slowly, watching the water, red-tinted with sunset and shimmering with the oily residue of decomposing plant life, as it washed over his boots. Servomotors labored to steady his balance. A reflection of the moon quivered in the current to his left like the image of a lidded eye. He thought of Zoe's eyes, eyes shocked by the loss of her thymostat, newborn, wide but wary. Understanding at last the price she had paid for her sanity.

He remembered how she had felt beneath him, crying out with what might have been, God help her, her first shared orgasm. She had trembled like this bridge. Afterward he had felt faintly ashamed, as if he had taken advantage of her, forced the living heart of her out of a complex membrane of defenses.

He trudged up the far bank of the Copper with gluey mud clinging to his boots. The sky was darker now, the forest a black corridor. Fallen logs rotted along the riverbank, and to his right he saw some small animal hesitate in the beam of his helmet lamp, then dash into the undergrowth.

When he had passed some meters into the woods and was enclosed in the space carved out of the darkness by his helmet light, his radio crackled once and fell silent. This would not have been unusual, except that he had asked his armor to screen all messages unless they arrived on Zoe's standard or emergency frequencies. In his exhaustion, it took him a moment to understand that this was what he had been waiting for.

Her signal must be weak. Obstructed by some obstacle perhaps,

or they would have heard her back at Yambuku. He stood still in
the midst of the forest, his boots sinking a little into the muddy
path—he might lose her if he moved—and thumbed his own com
controls. "Zoe? Zoe, it's Tam Hayes. Can you hear me?"

No answer.

He waited sixty seconds—an eternity, the cat's-eye moon sliding through the branches of the trees—and tried again.

This time her carrier frequency crackled alive and he heard her
voice, eerily close, but confused, as if he had wakened her from a
deep sleep. *"Theo?"*

"No, Zoe, it's Tam. I'm coming for you, but I need to know
where you are and how you're doing."

"Inside . . ." she murmured.

"Say again?"

"I'm inside a mound. Underneath. Under the ground."

"Inside which mound, Zoe?"

"I don't know. I think they're all connected. It's dark here."

He didn't like the way she sounded—weak, uncertain, almost
delirious. But it was her voice. She was alive. "Zoe, how are you?
Are you hurt?"

"How am I?" She was silent for a long moment. "Hot. It's hot
here. I can't see."

"Have they hurt you?"

"The diggers aren't here. Not always, I mean."

"Zoe, hang on. I'm coming to get you. Keep talking."

But he lost contact with her as he started toward the next ridge.

As he walked through the night he caught fragments of Zoe's
carrier frequency, never long enough to rouse her attention.

For all its exquisitely tuned servomotors and ergonomic flourishes, the bioarmor had grown terribly heavy around him. He was
aware of the enormous effort he expended carrying himself upslope
as he approached the foothills of the Coppers, where the soil grew
stony and he could turn, if he wished, and see the western plains
unfolding under moonlight toward the distant sea. Without a de-

fensive perimeter of tractibles and remensors he feared an attack from some large predator, but no such animal approached him; he was a formidable creature himself, he supposed, and his armor didn't smell like food.

He contacted Yambuku once, to tell them that Zoe was alive and he had spoken to her. Dieter Franklin was manning the comm console. "Tam," he said, "that's good news, but we have problems."

Hayes debated cutting the connection. There was only one problem he could deal with now, and that was the problem of Zoe. But Dieter was a friend, and Hayes let him talk.

"Your telemetry, for one. We have motors running hot in your left leg assembly. It's not critical yet, you can scroll the diagnostics if you haven't already, but it's not a good sign. What you need to do, Tam, is to turn around and hope you get close enough to Yambuku that we can send one of the reserve tractibles to carry you back, if need be. We can try to do something about Zoe from orbit. The IOS has a few landable remensors it can launch."

Hayes digested this information slowly. An overheating servo in his left leg . . . that would explain the extra weight he seemed to carry when he moved that foot, his tendency to list to port when his attention lapsed. But that wasn't bad, considering Dieter's first prediction that he would never reach the river. As for rescuing Zoe—

He said, "From orbit?"

"Because we're evacuating Yambuku. The seals are lapsing faster than we can replace them, and our stores are running low. On top of that, Theophilus says the IOS is getting cagey with him; maybe something's gone bad up there, too. We're looking at a last shuttle lift in forty-eight hours."

"Not enough time."

"That's the point. I'm trying to make your case with Theophilus. But he's giving the orders, and he's just about angry enough to write you off."

"He wants Zoe back." Her corpse, at least, Hayes did not add.

"Not as much as he wants to get off Isis. He's Family and he's very much in charge, but I think underneath all that he's starting to get seriously frightened."

"Thank you for the information, Dieter. Keep the core sterile. I'll be back."

He cut the connection before Dieter could respond.

Forty-eight hours.

If he started back now, he might make it.

TWENTY-ONE

"TAM? TAM ?"

The voice had come. The voice had gone. Unless she had imagined it. It was easy to imagine things, here in the overheated dark.

The digger, coiling its multijointed body in a sinuous circle, had also come and gone. The digger had broken the membrane of her excursion suit, slitting it from sternum to crotch with one razor-sharp claw, but carefully, drawing only a little blood. And then it had left her alone. To die, she had assumed, and she burned her firefly lamps recklessly, examining her body, waiting for the inevitable collapse of heart, lungs, liver, brain—because she was exposed at last to the Isian biosphere, microbes implanted beneath her skin by the animal's filthy claw. But her blood had dried quickly in the hot, close air. Daubs of it congealed on her fingers. She did not sicken and she did not die.

She did, however, exhaust her supply of firefly lamps, simply because she had dreaded dying in the dark. As the last lamp burned, she had willed herself to die before it blinked out. But she did not die. Only passed out for a time, or slept.

And then was horribly awake again, confined in this lightless hole.

She tore off her air filter, because there was no reason now not to breathe the Isian air directly; at best, it might hasten her inevitable death.

And still, *still*, she did not die.

The impulse to escape, a kind of smoldering panic, overwhelmed her once more. She resigned herself to the darkness; it was only a matter of using her other senses, Zoe told herself, of making maps in her head. Once again she crawled out of her cul-de-sac into a tunnel. She felt, but could not see, the mossy alien growths pressed against her exposed stomach, her breasts.

She crawled for an inestimable time, made several turns, tried to picture the labyrinth she had navigated as a map on parchment, an ancient mariner's map, but the map dissolved in the heat and confusion; she couldn't hold on to it.

She turned a corner and put her hand forward and touched the body of a digger. She froze in place, but the animal was evidently sleeping. Its fat, hollow scales, so useful for insulation, were splayed apart, radiating heat rather than conserving it. Without her air filter, the digger smelled pungent and close. The smell reminded her of a freshly manured farm field.

Zoe backed away. There wasn't room to turn around in the narrow tunnel. She dreaded what she might encounter with her feet, dreaded discovering that her world had been reduced to a few yards of excavated subsoil, while her body stubbornly and stupidly refused to die.

She had thrown away her filter mask but retained the excursion suit's headgear, and she was thankful for that when Tam Hayes spoke to her. Even if he was a hallucination, a fever dream, as she suspected he must be. It didn't matter. She drank the sound of him like cool water.

．　　　．　　　．

For a time she was in Tehran, carrying laundry under the stars.

She had been given the job as punishment for some transgression she couldn't remember, gathering the fetid, too-often-recycled smocks from the youngest inmates and carrying them in a plastic crate across the empty courtyard to the laundry shed—this in winter, and often late at night.

Her secret revenge was that she did not very much dislike the punishment. Distasteful as it was, because the younger children often soiled themselves or were ill, she relished the few free minutes under an open sky. Even in the cold, even in the dark. Perhaps especially then. The cold night air seemed somehow cleaner than the day's, as if it had been carried by benevolent winds from a distant glacier. And the coldest nights were often the clearest. The stars shone above the pallid lights of the camp with all the purity of their fixed, indifferent light. Light born in fire and older than the seas. She was in this place by mistake; she had been made for the stars, and she yearned to join them in their cycles, as aloof as ancient kings.

Some nights she put down her fetid burden and stole a moment all her own, shivering and gazing at the sky.

She was there now. In the camp. Or among the stars. One or the other. She was hungry and confused.

But what if, Zoe thought reluctantly, what if she traveled to the stars and found nothing there but more mud and dismal heat and deadly cold and sickness and strangers who didn't care whether she lived or died? What if she traveled all the way to the stars only to be buried in a hole in some alien ground?

What if, what if, what if?

Some nights she imagined that the stars could talk. She imagined that if she listened hard enough she would hear their voices, speaking a language as crisp and hard and colorful as gemstones.

She waited patiently to hear that timeless language and finally to understand it.

．　　　．　　　．

"Zoe!"

The voice again. Tam Hayes. Not the voice of the stars. But *he* was from the stars, wasn't he? Or at least from the Kuiper Belt, where people spoke more freely than they did on Earth.

"Zoe, can you hear me?"

The functioning part of her headgear kept the line open, waiting for a response. She licked her lips. Her lips were dry. She had finished the last of the suit's distilled water. Lately, in fact, she had taken to licking sour condensation from the damp ceiling of the tunnel.

"Tam," she croaked.

"Zoe, I'm half a kilometer from the digger mounds. I want to try to triangulate your position. Are you currently in a safe place?"

Well, no, she was *not* in a safe place, but she took his intended meaning. "I don't have to move. Not right away."

"Good. I'm coming for you."

"I don't think you can find me." She shook her head. "It's dark here."

"I understand that, Zoe. I'm coming."

"Dark and close."

The com connection crackled with static. Hayes asked, "What's your physical condition?"

That was a difficult question to answer. She could not, of course, see herself. She had to rely on sensation, on touch. But first things first. "I'm contaminated. The excursion membrane is damaged. I'm breathing unfiltered air."

There was no immediate answer. She imagined the dismay on his face, his mouth sagging at the corners. Would he cry for her? She might have cried herself if she hadn't been so dry.

"But I'm alive," she added.

"You're better protected than you think. Avrion Theophilus says you have a heavily augmented immune system—little wetpack nano colonies monitoring your blood. It's an untested system, but it seems to be working."

Zoe thought about that. A D&P immune system. That would

explain why she hadn't died with her first unfiltered breath of this awful, stagnant air.

But Theo would have told her, wouldn't he?

Theo wouldn't have kept a secret like that. It was Theo, after all, who had rescued her from the orphan crib, when all her clonal sisters had slowly sickened and died.

She must have said at least some of this aloud, because Hayes responded. "Zoe, were you ever sick during that time in Tehran?"

She considered the question. Weak, yes; malnourished, certainly; numbed and frightened, always. But the fevers had left her alone, even the Brazzaville 3 that had sickened so many inmates that Zoe had been drafted into carrying bedpans, and eventually, bodies.

Theo had saved her.

Theo. Theo. Or maybe Theo had saved her before she even left the crèche. Maybe Theo had given her something to protect her.

But then why had her sisters died, each in her own way? They were a clonal pod, after all. Identical, at least genetically. Unless they were different *inside*. Different augmentation. Different immune packages. That was how they did it with clonal animals: perform various modifications on genetically identical mice. . . .

Then place them in a hostile environment.

See who survives.

One of my girls survived.

Bad thought, Zoe scolded herself. Bad, bad thought.

She called out for Tam, but the link was broken again.

Time passed. She couldn't guess how much.

She was increasingly aware of the diggers, a great number of them by the sound, moving closer to her. She disliked the sound and the smell and the implicit threat. The noise drove her down the tunnel, where she fled by touch and by ear, scuttling in the dark until the digger-sounds were lost behind her, and resting only then, only then.

She knew they could have caught her if they wanted her. They were astonishingly fast and flexible in these tunnels of theirs. She presumed they did not want her, that they were ignoring her, that she was fleeing their ordinary and customary congregations.

But all the tunnels she followed seemed to bend gradually but steadily downward, until it came to her, a very bad thought indeed, that she was being gently herded deeper and deeper still into these vaults, farther and farther from the light.

TWENTY-TWO

"S<small>IR</small>." A<small>MRIT</small> S<small>EEGER</small>, the junior communications chief, actually trembled in Degrandpre's presence. Degrandpre had become so vigilant of infection that he had first mistaken the man's shaking and sweating for fever. But it was only his dread of authority. Of Degrandpre's magisterial power, such as it was. "Sir, I can't *do* that."

Degrandpre had come to the communications chamber personally. It was not a place he had often visited. Something about it appalled him, seemed antiquated and too large, all these winking glass appurtenances set into the wall like the monitor lamps of a seagoing battleship. The equipment in this room was perhaps the greatest technological achievement of the Devices and Personnel grandees, even greater in its way than the Higgs launches, maintaining a coherent and stable particle-pair link across hundreds of light years—the Grail of simultaneity in a relativistic universe. A link to Earth. The voice of the Families themselves emanated from this room.

But it was a fragile link, narrow in bandwidth, a bottleneck. Degrandpre had invoked information triage often enough in the past, usually to make his custodial work aboard the IOS appear as efficient as possible. Now he had elected to close down the link entirely. This room was too close to the encroaching perimeter of contagion.

"Sir," the engineer quavered, "they don't even know—back home, I mean—they don't know about the breach of Quarantine. We can't break the link, certainly not before we generate a distress call."

"And if we do that," Degrandpre said, "what do you imagine would happen? We're contaminated with an infectious agent that the Trusts would happily kill us all to contain. There won't be a rescue mission, certainly not if we're idiotic enough to broadcast a distress call."

The engineer blinked at this logic. Trembling, Degrandpre imagined, under the weight of blasphemy. "Sir, the regulations—"

"Regulations are suspended for the duration of the emergency." Degrandpre put his hand on the grip of his quirt, to make the matter official.

The engineer swallowed hard and left the communications chamber.

Alone in the room, Degrandpre located the main power switches—a bank of breakers that queried and recognized his thumbprints—and cut power to the complex of communications machineries embedded in the walls. Panels of indicator lights winked out. But that was not enough, not nearly enough.

He opened a deckplate over the phalanx of batteries (a battery of batteries, he thought senselessly) that provided a constant flow of uninterruptible current to the core of the particle-pair reactor, maintaining the delicate cohesion that was the beating heart of the link. He disconnected the cells manually, systematically, ignoring the alarm signals, until the overhead lights flickered and went dark in a last futile attempt to reroute power and preserve cohesion.

Degrandpre switched on a hand lamp.

Working by lamplight, he pulled the three coaxial lines that were the link's last source of energy. Deep in the supercooled com core, photons that had resonated with their Terrestrial twins for years began to decohere; information was scattered in a sudden entropic collapse, and the IOS was alone.

The Isis Orbital Station maintained a semblance of life. Shipments of replacement parts from the lunar Turing factories arrived with clockwork regularity, docked at the few remaining live bays and transferred their cargo to waiting tractibles. The station's holds filled with finished goods and raw materials that would never be put to use.

Of the nearly one thousand crew who had escaped quarantine, fifteen at most would find a berth on the sole escape vessel: a small Higgs sphere embedded by Turing tractibles in a cometary body and parked at an Isian Lagrange point. Fifteen, coincidentally, was the number of section managers plus Kenyon Degrandpre, the general manager. Two of the original section managers, including Corbus Nefford, had been lost to disease or general quarantine. Their replacements were guaranteed a berth.

Degrandpre understood the possibility of insurrection from the excluded crew, and indeed he had found his hand straying to the holster of his quirt more often in the last few days. But most of the crew were Terrestrial and sufficiently disciplined to carry on even in the face of this disaster. Degrandpre had encouraged them to believe in the possibility of rescue and they seemed grateful for the lie.

Once he had ordered the preparation of the escape launch, a sort of numb quiescence overtook the station. Degrandpre spent the last night in his cabin with a guard detail posted at the door, his first uninterrupted sleep in seventy-two hours. He dreamed of a steel labyrinth with shrinking corridors, and then of his father's greenhouses, dewy and warm in the winter afternoons.

Odd, he thought, waking to the chime of his scroll, how the psyche salvages calm from disaster. Dreamlike, these nautilus chambers of normalcy, when the IOS was in fact a crippled and doomed environment. The crisis was acute but somehow lazy, the way a sailing vessel damaged belowdecks betrays itself first with the gentlest of lists.

The scroll chimed again, an incoming message tagged high-priority. He debated ignoring it. What could be urgent when the end of everything was already in progress? He was facing, at best, a life in exile among the Kuipers. He could never return to a vengeful Earth, nor even to Mars, with its prisons and its extradition treaties. He wasn't a criminal—or so he insisted to himself—but the Families would see it differently. The Families would hang him, given a chance.

He picked up the scroll, his fingers suddenly numb with dread.

"Sir." It was Leander of Medical. "We have a stack of calls from Yambuku demanding immediate evacuation. Avrion Theophilus wants to speak to you directly."

And the last thing Kenyon Degrandpre wanted was some Family cousin pulling rank on him. God, not now. "Tell Theophilus I can't take his call. But clear them for the evacuation."

"And dock them—?"

"At the last Turing bay. And declare quarantine. Keep them in the shuttle, if possible."

"You mean—indefinitely?"

Yes, indefinitely; more precisely, until the escape module was launched—did he have to spell this out? "Is there anything else?"

"Yes." Leander's voice grew flat. "Reports of sickness in the Delta pod." A dormitory pod adjoining Engineering. "We sealed the bulkheads at once, of course, but—"

He shrugged.

Degrandpre understood the rest.

No guarantees.

TWENTY-THREE

THE OUTER RING of the ground station was hot, according to nanosensors embedded in the walls. Yambuku had lost its first perimeter of defense. Wholesale failure, Dieter Franklin insisted, could not be far behind.

Avrion Theophilus took the planetologist to the small launch-control room above the core—"the aerie," Franklin called it—to discuss their options.

Dieter Franklin had the slightly mad look of a man condemned to death. Condemned, and resigned to it. He spoke too freely. But Theophilus listened.

"There have been sporadic seal failures since the ground stations were first constructed. But nothing like this. We're looking at a massive, concentrated attack." The planetologist frowned. "Think of Isis as a killer. She wants in. She wants *us*. Until now, she's been fumbling with a set of keys, chemical compounds, trying to find one that fits the lock. It was a long and frustrating effort and it led us to believe we were relatively safe. But now she has the key. The killer has the key, and all she has to do is use it, patiently open the doors one by one, because it's too late to change the locks." He summarized: "Basically, we're fucked."

"So you agree that we ought to evacuate."

"It's the only way we can continue to draw breath." He took a drink from a cup of coffee—that bitter substance the station crew was pleased to call coffee. "However, we have two people in the field."

"Hayes."

"Tam Hayes and Zoe Fisher. Last I heard, she was still alive."

"Trapped under the digger mounds."

"Admittedly."

"By your own logic, we can't do any more for them without putting us all at risk."

"We're already just about as 'at risk' as a human being can get. That's not the point, sir."

"I've already demanded evac and I've already offered to monitor their situation from orbit. Give me another recommendation."

"We're obliged to take as many people out of harm's way as we can. So we evacuate the station, but we leave it up and running. Nanos and tractibles can monitor the core for at least a few days. We can maintain contact with Hayes from the IOS, and if by some miracle he or Zoe make it back to Yambuku we can send the shuttle for them. I wouldn't care to calculate the odds on any of this succeeding. But it costs us nothing."

Theophilus cupped his hands. "You call Isis 'she.' She wants in, you said. Do you have any idea *why* she wants in?"

The tall planetologist shrugged. "Maybe she's curious. Or maybe she's hungry."

Theophilus's scroll chimed; he glanced at it. A summons from the communications room. He headed for the door.

"Sir?" Dieter Franklin said.

Theophilus looked over his shoulder. "I'll consider your recommendation, Mr. Franklin. For now, the matter is closed."

TWENTY-FOUR

TAM HAYES, HIS left foot dragging and his servomotors flashing yellow overheat warnings in his corneal display like slow fireworks, arrived at the clearing around the digger mounds.

Sunlight came out of the hazy east with a humid intensity. The forest canopy breathed vapor like a sleepy dragon. Trails of fog wound down from the high Copper Mountain range in ghostly rivers.

Hayes moved cautiously in his ponderous bioarmor. At least five diggers (and more, perhaps, hidden in the tree perimeter or away from the mounds) watched him enter the clearing. He carried attached to his armor an electric quirt and a pistol loaded with rubberized bullets. So far, however, the diggers had maintained a respectful distance from him. They seemed neither alarmed nor hostile—only watchful. If, that is, he was interpreting their poised silences correctly. Their heads swiveled like radar dishes. Standing erect, they reminded Hayes of photographs he had seen: prairie dogs taking the sun. Sunlight glittered on their blank eyes.

He had kept open his channel to Zoe. She did not speak often, often ignored his calls, but he was comforted by the faint sound of her breathing.

The recent rain had softened the ground here, too. He saw a great number of digger tracks leading into and out of the low mound openings. He examined several of the mounds until he found a distinctive double groove in the drying mud, a track that might have been left by the heels of Zoe's excursion outfit if she had been dragged inside by her wrists.

Somewhere down there—down that slanting ramp into this warren of ancient excavations—somewhere down there was Zoe.

He was equipped with weapons and a powerful helmet lamp. He would gladly have followed.

But there was no way his bulky bioarmor would fit through that narrow hole.

He called Yambuku and asked for Avrion Theophilus.

Dieter Franklin came on first. He briefed Hayes on the situation at Yambuku: loss of shell integrity, the sterile core threatened, evacuation imminent "if those assholes on the IOS would pay attention to us for a fucking minute." By the time Hayes and Zoe reached the downstation, it would almost certainly be empty. "But we'll leave the light on for you. As long as the core is still sterile—and it ought to last a few days more—you can radio the IOS for a pick-up. Understand, Tam?"

"Put a candle in the window for us, Dieter."

"Count on it."

"Now hand me to Theophilus."

Master Avrion Theophilus announced his presence on-line. Hayes said, "I have a question for you, Theo."

He imagined Theophilus wincing at the name. Zoe called him Theo, but Zoe was privileged, his surrogate daughter. Technically,

Hayes ought to address him as "Master Theophilus." Theo was a good Family man.

"Speak," Theophilus said.

"Zoe's been talking now and then. I don't believe you picked up any of this at Yambuku. She has a limited radio perimeter."

"Correct."

"She's lucky to have those immune enhancements, Theo. They're the only thing keeping her alive."

"Lucky indeed. Make your point, Mr. Hayes."

"She's just curious, Theo . . . you being sort of a father to her and all. When she went into that orphan crib, did she already have this blood gear?"

There was a pause. The silence, Hayes supposed, of Theo's conscience. "Yes, she did, as a matter of fact. That may be what helped her survive."

"But not her clone sisters."

"Her clonal sisters had been fitted with other forms of augmentation."

"So it was an experiment. Put five rats in a cage and give them all smallpox, that sort of thing."

"Considering your situation, Mr. Hayes, I'll forgive the judgmental tone. The Tehran facility would not have been my first choice for the girls. Political circumstances forced our hand. However, yes, her confinement there ultimately served a scientific purpose."

"She thinks you rescued her. You might as well have raped her yourself."

"What we're discussing is a Family matter. You should have abandoned this kind of moral high-handedness when you left the Kuipers. Family values aren't open to question."

"Give the microphone back to Dieter," Hayes said. "Theo."

More of the diggers came out of the shadows now, though they continued to give Hayes a wide berth. He hoped not to anger them.

They might take their revenge on Zoe—if they were capable of such thoughts.

Dieter Franklin came on-line again, belatedly. "You're just making trouble for yourself, Tam."

"I have plenty already. Theo still listening?"

"Master Theophilus has left the communication room, if that's what you mean. But this conversation is a matter of record."

"Dieter, I have a question. The bioarmor—it's sort of a miniature downstation, right? I mean, it has a series of perimeters around a sterile core."

"In a way. Big shell for the heavy processing and to house the servomotors, gel insulation under that; at the bottom a layer of primary containment about as thick as your skin."

"So how much of it can I take off?"

"Say again, Tam?"

"How much of this armor can I strip and still have any kind of protection?"

The silence this time was longer. Hayes looked again at the mound entrance before him. Dark as a badger hole. Narrow as a sewer pipe.

"Conservatively," Dieter said, "none. It doesn't work that way."

"Answer the question."

"I'm not an engineer. I'll get Kwame in here if you like."

"You know this gear as well as Kwame does."

"I take no responsibility—"

"I'm not asking you to. The responsibility is all mine. Answer the question."

"Well . . . if you strip off the hard shell, you probably won't die immediately. You'd need the helmet, though for the air scrubbers. And you'd be standing there in a plastic wrapper about as strong as aluminum foil. Best case, it might hold off the native microorganisms for a couple of hours before you go hot. If you scrape your elbow, of course, all bets are off. Tam, this is a fundamentally stupid idea."

"I need to go in after her."

"Both of you will die."

"As may be," Hayes said. He hands were already on the latches of his boots.

Dieter Franklin caught up to Avrion Theophilus in the hallway outside the comms room. "Master Theophilus, I want to apologize on behalf of Tam Hayes."

"It's not your apology to make, Mr. Franklin."

"Sir, I trust this won't interfere with our plans. That is, if he does make it back to Yambuku somehow, we *will* send a shuttle for him . . . won't we?"

"Family business," Theophilus said briskly. "You needn't worry about it."

TWENTY-FIVE

ALONE IN THE sooty courtyard of the orphan crib, Zoe listened to the winter stars.

She listened with her eyes closed, because she couldn't see. She listened with her arms at her sides, because her arms were too heavy to move. She breathed through her mouth, because the air was thick and stank of strange animals.

Maybe she wasn't in the courtyard at all . . . but here were the stars, voices like a faraway church choir on a cold night, voices like a train whistle bent across a prairie. Voices like snowflakes whispering at a bedroom window. Voices like the yellow light that shines out of the homes of strangers.

It was good not to be alone. Zoe shivered with the fever that had lately overtaken her and tried to focus on the sound of the stars. She knew she was eavesdropping on a vast and impossibly ancient conversation, none of it quite comprehensible but all of it radiant with significance, a foreign language so complex and so lovely that it exuded meaning the way a blossom drips nectar.

There was a closer voice too, but that one was more disturbing, because that voice spoke to her directly, spoke with the voice of her own memories, touched her and marveled at her, just as she marveled at the stars.

"T am?"

"I'm coming," he said. He said it more than once. And something else. Something about her excursion gear. Her tool kit.

She found it difficult to pay attention. She would rather listen to the stars.

She said once, mistakenly, "Theo?" Because she was back in the orphan crèche again, a dream.

"No," Hayes said. "Not Theo."

The nearest voice was warm and enclosing, and it came to her disguised as a memory of Dieter Franklin.

Here was the gangly planetologist right in front of her, lit from within, his ribs and elbows obvious even under the rough blue Yambuku service uniform. "This is the answer," he told Zoe eagerly, "the answer to all those old questions. We're not alone in the universe, Zoe. But we're damned near unique. Life is almost as old as the universe itself. Nanocellular life, like the ancient Martian fossils. It spread through the galaxy before Earth was born. It travels on the dust of exploded stars."

This was not really Dieter talking, but some other agent talking to Zoe through her memory of Dieter. She knew that. It might have been frightening. But she wasn't afraid. She listened carefully.

"I would explain this to you more fully, little one, but you don't have the words. Look at it this way. You're a living, conscious entity. And so are we all. But not in the same way. Life flourishes everywhere in the galaxy, even in the hot and crowded core of it, where the ambient radiation would kill an animal like yourself. Life is supple and adaptable. Consciousness arises . . . well, almost everywhere. Not your kind of consciousness, though. Not animals, born in ignorance and living for a brief time and dying forever. That's the peculiarity, not the rule."

"I can hear the stars talking," Zoe said.

"Yes. We all can, all the time. They're mostly planets, not stars. Planets such as Isis. Often very different physically, but all of them filled with life. All of them talking."

"But not Earth," Zoe divined.

"No. Not Earth. We don't know why. The grain of life that found your sun must have been damaged in some way. You grew wild, Zoe. Wild and alone."

"Like an orphan."

Dieter—the Dieter-thing—smiled sadly. "Yes. Exactly like an orphan."

But it wasn't really Dieter talking.

It was Isis.

"Zoe, the beacon."

This was Tam's voice, his radio voice.

She opened her eyes reflexively but saw nothing. Sweat ran in itchy courses down her forehead and her cheeks. Her mouth was ridiculously dry, as dry as wood, her tongue thick and clumsy.

"Zoe, can you hear me?"

She croaked an acknowledgment. Her stomach hurt. Her feet were numb. She was as cold as she had ever been, colder than on the coldest winter night in Tehran, colder than the core of a Kuiper body spinning through space. Her sweat was cold, and the salt of it burned her eyes. She tasted it on her cracked lips.

"Zoe, I need you to listen to me. Listen to me."

She nodded uselessly, imagining for a moment that she was blind and he was here with her. But that was only his radio voice.

"Zoe, you should have an RF beacon on your tool belt. The RF beacon, Zoe, remember? On your tool belt. About the size of a personal scroll. Can you activate it?"

The radio beacon. But why? He knew she was here. They could even talk.

"I can't find you without a little help. Activate the beacon and I can follow it."

Her signal bouncing off the positioning satellites, talking back to Tam's helmet. Yes, that would work. Wincing, she reached around her torn excursion suit, exploring the tool belt with her fingers. Her fingers were as awkward as parade balloons, and there was moss slime, or something, all over her torso. She expected the beacon to have been lost in all her useless crawling, but no, here it was, a small box, slippery when it came out of its holster.

"I have it," she managed. Crude, her human voice.

"Can you activate it for me?"

She fumbled with the device until she found the indentation on the side. She touched it repeatedly until the beacon came to life.

It chirped—one small sound to let her know it was working. And a light came on, a tiny red indicator on the face of the unit.

Small as it was, it was nevertheless a light. Zoe held it up to her face, basking in the sensation of vision. Faint, precious spark! It illuminated, if poorly, anything within a centimeter or so of the beacon. Beacon indeed.

She put her hand next to the light.

She didn't like what she saw.

"Got it," Tam said. "Loud and clear. Hang on, Zoe. Not long now."

The stars—or at least their planets—were alive and had been talking to themselves (singing to themselves, Zoe understood) for billions of years.

Isis, disguised as her memory of Dieter Franklin, sang her a soothing song. A nursery song. Something her nannies had once sung to her, a silly rhyme about the seashore. If you put a shell to your ear you can hear the sea.

Consciousness, Isis told her, is born in the small things of the universe, though no small thing is itself conscious. The trick life learned, Isis explained, was to sustain a ghostly contact when one

cell divided into two, a quantum equivalency of electron pairs suspended in microtubules, "like the particle-pair link that connects
you to Earth."

Life invented it first, Zoe thought, like so many other things.
Like eyes: turning photon impacts into neurochemical events with
such subtlety that a frog can target a fly and a man can admire a
rose. We *see* the stars, after all, Zoe thought. We just can't *hear*
them.

Animal consciousness, Isis said, is a rare event in the universe.
Cherished for its rarity. The galactic bios welcomed home its orphans. Isis was sad that so many had died needlessly—brief flickers
here of Macabie Feya, Elam Mather—but that was unpreventable,
an autonomic reflex of the Isian bios; an action as involuntary as
the beating of Zoe's heart, and just as difficult to moderate. But Isis
was doing her best.

"I'm not dead," Zoe noted.

"You're different, little one."

Different enough to survive?

One of my girls survived.

Isis was silent on the subject.

TWENTY-SIX

TOO LATE, KENYON Degrandpre thought.

He marched, head high, down the ring corridor of the crippled IOS.

Too late.

Look at me, he thought. Look at me in my uniform, crisp and neat. The ring corridor was virtually empty—large numbers of the crew had elected to die discreetly, in their cabins—but the few he passed still regarded him with a frightened deference. His hand was on his quirt, just in case. But the enlightened manager seldom stoops to corporal punishment.

He walked stiffly, formally, toward the last of the docking bays, where the escape vehicle waited to take him away from the IOS, to the Higgs vessel. He was conscious of his footsteps, rhythmic and proportioned. He did not veer to the left or to the right. He walked in the middle of the ring corridor, its corrugated walls equidistant from his braced shoulders. He slouched only at the low bulkhead doors.

He passed through a section of crew quarters. Each crewman had private quarters, cloistered steel cubicles hardly larger than university carrels and equipped with folding beds. Some of these doors were open, and in some of the rooms Degrandpre passed he saw men and women inert on their cots, blood crusting on their noses and lips. Occasionally he heard a moan, a scream. Most of the doors were closed. Most of the crew had chosen to perish in privacy.

"Slow," Corbus Nefford had called this disease. Slow in its incubation perhaps, by the yardstick of Isian microorganisms. But not in its final effect. From first symptoms to death, three or four hours might elapse. Not more.

The survivors he passed wore a blank, shocked look. They had not died, but expected to; or believed against all reason in some imminent rescue, a miraculous reversal of fate.

But Degrandpre believed in that, too. He found himself finally unable to contemplate the possibility of his own death. Not when he had gone to such obscene lengths to prevent it: the multiple quarantines, the killing of the Marburg evacuees, the breaking of the particle-pair link to Earth. No: In the end he *must* survive, else all was meaningless.

To that end he modulated his steps and crossed the thick steel threshold of the emergency dock with an apparent calm. Only the sweat rolling down his cheeks betrayed him. The sweat bothered him, as his physical weakness bothered him. If he wasn't ill, was he mad? Was illness madness?

He arrived shortly after the appointed time and was disappointed to find only three of his senior managers waiting in the prep room, a small chamber linked directly to the escape vessel. Leander, Solen, and Nakamura. The others, Leander explained, were ill.

But we have escaped it, Degrandpre told them. The virus hasn't entered our bodies; or if it has, it has been weakened to such a degree that our bodies can defend themselves.

After all, he thought. Here I am.

He used his senior manager's key to unlock and activate the escape vehicle. The process was not dramatic. A heavy door slid open. Beyond it was the cramped interior of the escape craft, acceleration couches arrayed in a circle, no flight controls; this was a kind of enormous tractible, capable of one intelligent act, docking with the Higgs sphere.

Leander said, "I feel like a coward."

"There's no cowardice in this. There's nothing more for us to do."

Nakamura hesitated at the threshold. "Manager," she quavered, "I'm not well."

"None of us are *well*. Get in or stay out."

The escape vehicle lurched away from the IOS and followed a looping route to the Higgs launcher, waiting at the L-5 between Isis and her small moon.

The Higgs vehicle was embedded in an icy planetisimal, deposited here by a tractible tug some seven years ago. Remains of the tractible thrusters still dotted the object, blackened nozzles like rusty sculptures set in a dark stone garden. The wholly automated launch complex noted the proximity of the escape vehicle and negotiated docking protocols with it.

The smaller vessel docked successfully. Inside the planetisimal, lights flickered on in anticipation of human presence. Temperatures in its narrow corridors bumped up to twenty-one degrees centigrade. Medical tractibles lined up at the docking hatches in case of need.

The launch complex queried the escape module repeatedly, but received no intelligible answer.

After a time, as if disappointed by the nonappearance of an expected guest, the launch complex darkened itself once more. Habitat chambers cooled to ambient. Liquid water was returned to ice vessels for storage.

Supercooled processors clocked time with infinite patience. Isis prowled on in the orbit of its sun, and no human voices spoke.

TWENTY-SEVEN

TAM HAYES' HELMET light was good for at least a day and a half. More than likely, the lamp would outlast him, would continue to burn while his corpse cooled—or, perhaps, heated, nursing a furious brood of Isian microorganisms.

So far, however, he was intact.

He forced his way through the narrow digger tunnels. The sheer fragility of his stripped-down excursion armor and the size of his helmet obliged him to move slowly. He had been most afraid of an attack from the diggers—he was horribly vulnerable—but the animals had kept their distance outside and were nowhere visible inside the mound complex. There was, however, much evidence of their recent presence. He passed loculi and cul-de-sacs filled with food, carefully categorized—here a cache of seeds; there a mound of fruit fermenting in the heat. Down other tributary tunnels he saw motion just beyond the range of his lamp, a squirming that might have been sex, or birth, or child-rearing, or a barn dance.

He followed his beacon and kept his com link up, listening as Zoe's occasional monologues veered toward incoherency.

The Yambuku shuttle must have left for the obstinately silent IOS by now. Tam Hayes and Zoe Fisher were the last people on the continent. Outside the mound tunnels, over the long western steppes and the temperate forest and the spires of the Copper Mountain range, night was falling.

Despite her fever, despite her frequent lapses into unconsciousness, Zoe heard the voice of Isis more clearly now.

Heard it, or at least *understood* it. She knew (and she tried to tell Hayes, in her lucid moments) how the consciousness of Isis rode on the planet's bios; how every living cell, from the most ancient thermophyllic bacteria to the specialized cells in the black eye of a digger, hosted the entity Isis. Cells lived and died, evolved, formed communities, became fish and birds and animals; none of these things knew Isis or was controlled by Isis. Isis rode on their mechanism the way the contents of a book ride on the ink-stained leaves of paper.

"It's only," she whispered to Tam Hayes—to someone— Theo, perhaps—"it's only when animal consciousness reaches a certain complexity that Isis can interact with it. The diggers. They're not really very smart. They're ninety-percent animal. But they have a little bit of Isis in them. They can hear her, a little."

And:

"It's why none of the SETI projects ever found anything. The galaxy *is* full of life, and it *is* talking—oh God, Tam, if you could hear the voices! Old, old voices, older than Earth! But we couldn't listen. There's an Isis, but there's no Earth. Whatever spores of life fertilized Earth back when Earth was hot and new, they were broken—the *link* was broken, the quantum coherency life learned to carry between the stars was broken, lost. Earth grew wild and alone. When primates learned the trick of consciousness, of neurons talking to neurons the way planets talk to planets, making consciousness out of quantum events—when that happened, there was nothing to get in the way of our evolution, no Earth, only *Earthlings.*"

And hadn't she felt it? Hadn't she felt something of the kind when she carried the filthy laundry under the winter stars? This was wrong, all the torture and silences and hostility and the slaughterhouse of human history, this was wrong; but what was *right?* What was so dear and so utterly lost that she ached at the absence of it?

"Why do people worship gods, Tam?"

Because we're descended from them, Zoe thought. We're their mute and crippled offspring, in all our millions.

She coughed and felt the wetness of blood on her hand.

Somewhere in these catacombs of mud and dung, Tam Hayes was scrabbling toward her.

H ayes, listening to Zoe's babbling in the earpiece of his helmet, wondered how much of this she had picked up from Dieter Franklin. How much was her own delirium?

How much might even be true?

But there was too much of Zoe in it. She needed the idea of Isis, he thought, the idea of a community of worlds, because she had never been truly welcome in any world of her own. The crippled orphan was Zoe, not humanity.

This long tunnel, like a central corridor, coiled deeper into the earth. Hayes imagined a spiral carved into the stony darkness by countless generations of diggers. Veering around obstacles, lurching with idiot persistency toward the bedrock.

Water-rich, almost transparent plants thrived on the moisture at the tunnel's floor. Hayes wondered at their metabolism: lightless, mineral-driven. The plants gushed sticky fluid under the weight of his gloves.

Zoe's delusion. The sky talking to her. Well, he understood the feeling. He had looked at the stars often enough, had climbed up through the Red Thorn sun gardens to a port observatory and watched the sky wheeling around him, the sun no more than an especially bright star among all the carousel stars. That had been one of his mother's convictions, that the bios linked all things, from kangaroos to Martian microfossils. It was a religious belief, part of her Ice Walker upbringing. He had rejected it along with the rest of the Kuiper Belt's patchwork ideologies—half puritan, half libertine.

But he had believed it when he watched the stars. He knew what it was to feel meaning beyond the limit of his comprehension, the stars a vast city he could never enter, a republic in which he could never claim citizenship.

He felt a cool wetness under the arch of his left leg and knew abstractly that he must have compromised the delicate core of his protective membrane. Just like Zoe. But he didn't have her immune augmentation. He would have to hurry.

No need for caution now.

Maybe she could use his helmet to find her way out.

She was tempted to give up.

Isis couldn't save her—not her natural body, which was dying despite all her augmentation, under attack from too many unfamiliar microorganisms. She might have withstood a single infection, or two, or even three; but she was besieged now by organisms beyond number, weakened by hunger and thirst.

But Isis cherished her and would not let her go. Zoe—the pattern of her—could be sustained indefinitely in the dense matrix of the Isian bios. That was how Isis was talking to her, viral entities slipping into her nervous system, making fresh Isian cells out of Terrestrial neurons. Killing her, but remembering her. Imagining her. Dreaming her. Still, she waited for Tam.

When he reached her at last, he was deeply feverish.

He had forgotten, in all his desperate haste, why he was here—found himself aware only of the tunnel and its pressure on his knees and neck, the weight of soil above his head, the strangeness and the terror of it. And when that knowledge weighted too heavily, he would breathe slowly and fight the panic of confinement, the panic that threatened to overwhelm and suffocate him.

And when his hands ceased trembling and his legs regained the power of motion, he pressed on. Following the beacon leading him to Zoe.

Strange how she had come to mean so much to him, this Terrestrial orphan with a failed thymostat. How he had invested in her so many of his hopes and so much of his fear, and how she had led him into this labyrinth under Isis.

He imagined he was climbing, not crawling . . . that the brightness in the corridor before him was something more than the glare of his helmet lamp.

Zoe's vision was failing, along with her other functions, but she saw at least faintly Tam's light burning out of the darkness as he approached.

She blinked her eyes, a sticky sensation.

He knew when he saw her that what he had suspected was true: Zoe was beyond rescue.

The bios had been working hard at her.

She sat with her spine against the curved wall of the cul-de-sac, her excursion membrane as tattered as an old flag. There was dried blood on her belly, the color of sooty brick. Fungus had attacked her exposed skin, growing in swollen circles of blue or stark white.

Even the albino moss had begun to feed on her, rising to the moisture of her in lush, trailing fingers. Her boots were buried in it.

She watched him unlatch and remove his helmet. The beam of the helmet's lamp—so bright!—flashed wildly about the cul-de-sac. It shone on the ceiling of impacted clay and animal matter, on the gauzy insect web full of mummified husks, on the delicate bulbs of moss. He was offering his helmet to her, with all its rebreathing apparatus and water reserves and gaudy, glorious light.

The generosity of the act was heartbreaking.

But she waved away the gift. Too late, too late.

Hayes understood the gesture. He was saddened, but he set the helmet aside, its light aimed steadily now at the ceiling. With each breath he drew more Isian microorganisms into his lungs, not that it mattered. He summoned his strength and fit his body next to Zoe's in the cramped space of the alcove. No fear of contact now. Life touches life, as Elam used to say.

Heat radiated from Zoe, the heat of fever and the heat of parasitical infection. But her lips, when he touched them, were cool. Cool as the rim of a bucket of water drawn from a deep and mossy well.

He said, "I do hear them. The stars."

But she was past listening.

The diggers avoided their store of strange-smelling meat until it had decomposed into a more familiar mass of diffuse enzymatic tissues, ripe with life. The smell became rich, then exotic, then irresistible.

Coiling into the meat chamber, one by one and one after another, they feasted for days.

TWENTY-EIGHT

THE ISIS ORBITAL Station wheeled through its circuit of the planet, crippled but functional.

Spaceborne tractibles fetched water and oxygen from Turing extractors on the moon's icy poles, replacing the small but inevitable losses of recycling. Lately many human bodies had been discovered by the housekeeping tractibles, and these too had been recycled for their nutrients. Flush with fresh sources of nitrogen, phosphorous, potassium, and trace elements, the gardens thrived. Sun panels cast their glow on dense hedgerows of kale and lettuce, a bounty of tomatoes and cucumbers.

Avrion Theophilus had taken refuge in the gardens while the others died—Dieter Franklin, Lee Reisman, Kwame Sen, and everyone who had shuttled up from Yambuku, victims of the slow virus that had infiltrated the station.

The virus continued to tunnel through bulkhead seals in search of nourishment, but after a time, it found none; after a time, all its spores lay dormant.

Below, on the planet's surface, Marburg and Yambuku were deserted, and Theophilus had ignored the increasingly desperate pleas from the arctic outpost as its perimeters, too, were breached.

All dead now; and, to his horror, he had found the escape craft missing, the particle-pair link to Earth permanently broken.

And yet he lived.

He had insisted on traveling to Isis with the same immune-system modifications his Trust had given Zoe Fisher. The wetware protected him quite effectively from, at least, the single organism that had infiltrated the IOS.

He was alive, and likely to continue living. But he was alone.

He moved through the filtered light of the gardens, patrolling restlessly among the silent tractibles and succulent green leaves. He talked to himself, because there was no one else to talk to. He wondered aloud and repeatedly whether anyone would come, whether he would be rescued, or whether he would be left here; whether he would go mad after a month or a year of isolation, or whether his thymostat would keep him obstinately sane.

There would be time enough to know all the answers. Time and more time.

His shadow followed him through the corridors of the IOS like a lost dog.

He waited, but no one came.

EPILOGUE

FOR ONE HUNDRED and fifty years—almost to the month since its abandonment—the Isis Orbital Station navigated its rounds. Solar-powered (and still quite active despite the failure of nearly half its photon exchangers), self-monitoring, self-cleaning, it had waited with apparently infinite patience for its salvagers to arrive.

From a distance, it seemed unchanged. Up close, age and damage had left more obvious marks.

Jasmin Chopra was the first of the salvage crew to board the IOS. Terrestrial born, she could trace her lineage back through both Revolutions. One of her ancestors, Anna Chopra, had even been tried and executed as a provocateur after a long life of apparently dutiful service to *les Familles anciennes*.

But that wasn't why Jasmin was here. She was here because she had conducted two salveur crews through the deadly ruins of KB47 and reclaimed several tonnes of exotic-matter Higgs-lens fragments without a single casualty. She was older now—pushing fifty Terrestrial years—but she had volunteered early for the Isis mission and used her status for maximum leverage. And here she was, farther from home than human beings had been for a chaotic century and a half.

After the station's docking seals were judged intact and the internal pressure raised a couple of millibars, Jasmin Chopra became the first of the salveurs to cross the threshold.

She didn't fear contagion. She was equipped with a biostat capable of digesting, poisoning, dissolving, cauterizing, or otherwise killing any foreign material that chanced to enter her body. She shuddered, in fact, at the thought of the adventurers who had died here or on the planet's surface, their defenses against the Isian bios as frail as kites in a windstorm. Nor was she afraid of what she might find aboard the station. As she expected, any extant human remains had been tidied up by housekeeping tractibles and funneled into the nitrogen cycle. Given its history, the IOS was almost supernaturally clean.

Clean, but eerie. Everywhere there was evidence of life abandoned almost in mid-thought—clothing left where it had dropped, old-fashioned scrolls scattered on desktops, even loose paper documents fluttering in the ventilation drafts. Energy-starved tractibles mobbed her legs like lonesome puppies.

Her initial survey of the continuously pressurized portion of the IOS brought her at last to the tiered sun garden.

The agro tractibles had been diligent in their long tasks, but not much remained. The herb-and-spice aeroponics tanks must have lost power at some critical juncture. All they had lately raised was a crop of dust. On the larger and more complex vegetable tiers, everything had died but the kale and tomato plants. These had gone on, year after year, surviving draught and power failures, seeding themselves into the perpetually washed amalgam beds, growing yellow and reedy and brittle with the accumulating scarcity of micronutrients—but growing.

The persistence of life, Jasmin thought. How it gets *into* things.

.   .   .

The true wild lay below, on the planet's surface.

Jasmin wasn't the first to set foot there, however, even discounting the original research teams. That privilege was reserved for the young and photogenic: specifically, Jak and Elu Reys, twin Martian paleontologists who looked like lean angels as they took their first breath of Isian air, so full of strange new scents. The moment was recorded for broadcast back to its intended Terrestrial audience.

Jasmin left the shuttle after the others, a deferential act but also her preference. She was a salveur, not a scientist. Her concern was to see whether a new work station could be constructed from the weathered remains of Yambuku or whether it would be best to start from scratch. At least we have one advantage, she thought. We can walk in the open air, actually *touch* the planet. We're so profoundly augmented that we could even drink the local water— given a little judicious filtering of native toxins. We can, if need be, build log cabins and live like pioneers.

But for now she was content to slip down the shuttle ramp into a meadow of blowsy seed pods under a hot noon sky. A gusty wind plucked at her hair. For one euphoric moment she was tempted to shed her clothes and run naked into the reef of trees beyond the slope of this ridge. She was as impulsive as that poor treasonous ancestor of hers.

No one had spoken yet. The only sound was the wind. Wind turning the grasses in slow swells, wind out of the west and freshening.

She closed her eyes, and it seemed to Jasmin Chopra that she heard the sound of voices on the wind—a whisper of speechless conversation. We are here, she thought, and the wind whispered, *We are here.* This all seems somehow familiar, she thought, and the wind said, *We know you. We remember you.*

Strange.

She walked a little way across the meadow until she could see a part of the old Trust station, Yambuku, rising past the canopy of trees. Its shuttle-bay dome was cracked and covered with green creepers; it had been reclaimed by the wild.

A brittle echo of the human presence on Isis. The bios is strong, Jasmin thought. We have a lot to learn.